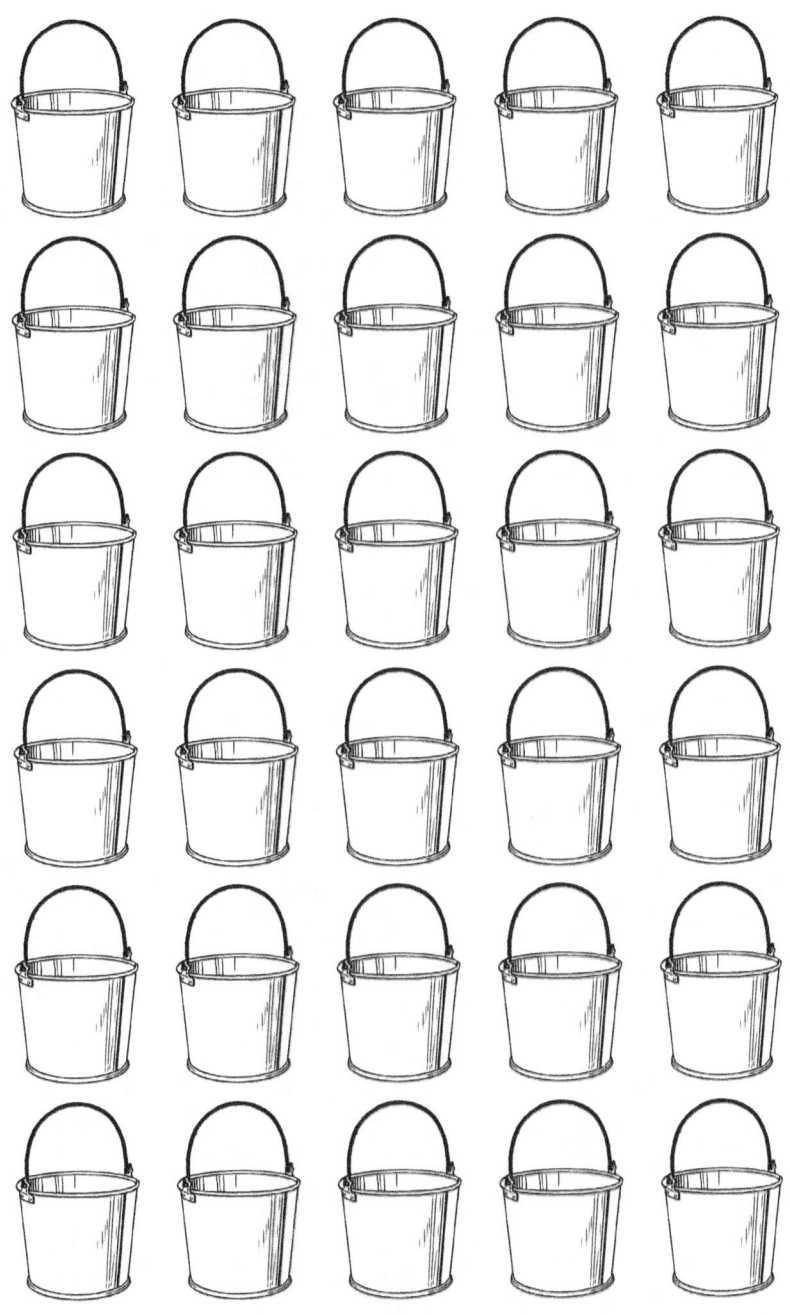

Pure Slush Books

2014

December

Vol. 12

a Pure Slush book

Pure
Slush

2014 December Vol. 12 is edited by Matt Potter and
published by Pure Slush, September 2014.

Cover photograph © Ned Horton
http://www.hortongroup.com

ISBN: 978−1−925101−56−0

You can find *Pure Slush* at http://pureslush.webs.com

Copies of all *Pure Slush* publications can be bought
at http://pureslush.webs.com/store.htm

All queries re *Pure Slush* can be made
via email to edpureslush@live.com.au

A note on differences in punctuation and spelling

Pure Slush proudly features (both online and in print) writers from all over the English−speaking world. Some speak and write English as their first language, while for others, it's their second or third or even fourth language. Naturally, across all versions of English, there are differences in punctuation and spelling, and even in meaning. These differences are reflected in the stories *Pure Slush* publishes, and it accounts for any differences in punctuation, spelling and meaning found within these pages.

stories by

Guilie Castillo—Oriard

Townsend Walker

Derek Osborne

Gloria Garfunkel

John Wentworth Chapin

Lynn Beighley

Andrew Stancek

Rachel Ambrose

Gill Hoffs

Susan Tepper

Jessica McHugh

Shane Simmons

Michelle Elvy

Len Kuntz

Michael Webb

James Claffey

Gwendolyn Joyce Mintz

Stephen V. Ramey

Gay Degani

Sally—Anne Macomber

Mandy Nicol

Margaret Bingel

Darryl Price

Teresa Burns Gunther

Matt Potter

Gary Percesepe

Nathaniel Tower

Kimberlee Smith

Vanessa Weibler Paris

Joanne Jagoda

h. l. nelson

for

Daniel Turner

again

because he has heard versions of these stories

over and over

M.P.

The Miracle of Small Things
by Guilie Castillo–Oriard

Monday, 1ˢᵗ December 2014

M onday nights are always crowded at De Heeren. Not a single empty table inside, not even on the patio. Familiar faces turn my way, hands raise, fingers wiggle hello. Nudges make more faces turn, even from tables full of strangers. *Look, Curaçao's crazy dog lady.* Too late for regrets. Not many places to pick from on a Monday, anyway.

The hostess gives me a bright smile. "Goeden avond," she says. "Inside or outside, Ms. Solak?"

Inside there's more light. Inside, the hum of conversation will cover awkward silences. Which begs the question: why should I care? "Outside," I say. Dagger of awkwardness, find thy sheath.

"Just five minutes while we set it up."

I wander over to the bar and make small talk, ignore the veiled once–overs the glitzy women give my jeans and my flip–flops, until the hostess taps my arm. "Your table is ready."

Dekko, the manager, is waiting outside, full of apologies. The table barely catches the edge of the patio lighting. In the darkness, its candle centerpiece hollers *romantic*. "I have better spots inside," he says.

And then I see him, striding into the restaurant with those long legs. His hair is longer, his shirt is untucked, the sleeves

15

rolled up, but it looks freshly ironed. His feet, though, are the key: the great Luis Villalobos is wearing *flip−flops* to a restaurant.

"It's okay, Dek. This is fine."

He says something about sending over a bottle of wine and I nod, say thanks (I think). Luis is scanning faces in the half−light. When he sees me, he grins, and it's that same arrogant hot−shot attitude. The flip−flops lie; he hasn't changed.

"I wasn't sure you'd come," he says as he sits down across from me.

I give him what I hope looks like a non−committal smile. "How are you?"

"Good. You?"

He looks happy. More relaxed even than in Bonaire that one luscious weekend. Maybe it's the tan, the weight he's lost. All that lugging around of tanks in the sun. "Enjoying your new career?"

He nods, looks down at the table. "So far, yeah."

"Being a dive instructor was a lifelong ambition?"

He laughs. "I'm not an instructor. And no, not remotely. But I do love it."

"So far." A gibe. I can't help myself.

He lets out his breath with a *whoosh*. "So far."

Where the hell is Dekko and the wine? A waiter at least, maybe some water? "How's Al?"

"Great." He smiles that tender, childish smile of his, the one that gave me faith in humanity. "Our neighbor has a Rottweiler puppy − well, not a real one, a mix, but he looks Rottweiler−ish − and he and Al totally hit it off."

"I'm glad he has company while you're working."

"Actually, he comes to work with me."

I want to frown, to show I disapprove − Al isn't exactly the world's most socialized dog, and Luis isn't going to win any trainer awards any time soon − but the sheer absurdity of the image trumps everything and makes me chuckle. "You bring your *dog* to work?"

16

He laughs. "Pretty awesome for the guy who didn't even like dogs, right?"

Pretty glib for the guy who was going to leave his dog behind is what I think. But I don't say it. Anger is nothing but hurt; revealing it makes us vulnerable. And I'm done being vulnerable. "Where are you living?"

"Montaña. Tiny place. Big yard, though, all walled in. At night the stars are amazing. And rent's affordable on my new salary."

Montaña? How far the great have fallen. "Is it safe, though?"

He chuckles. "I'm from Mexico City, remember? This island is the safest place on Earth."

"Don't get cocky, Luis. It's the —"

Dekko arrives with two bottles. "I have an Argentinian merlot and a Spanish tempranillo, both excellent. If you're having meat, I'd suggest —"

"We're not eating," I say, in English. "The merlot —"

"The tempranillo sounds good." Luis puts a hand on mine. An apology for interrupting, or is he marking territory for Dek — or me?

"Bit heavy, no?" I slide my hand away, disguise the movement by rummaging in my bag for my phone.

"This one's very light," Dek says, and for once I resent his solicitude. He does offer the half measure to me for tasting, which is somewhat appeasing.

"I wasn't being dismissive," Luis says as Dek moves away to check on another table. "I know it's not the best area, which is one of the reasons I bring Al with me to work. They want to break in, let them. There's nothing to steal. But Al wouldn't see it that way, and I don't want him to get hurt."

"You have savings. It doesn't have to be the lap of luxury, but —"

"It's not bad. You should come see for yourself sometime."

I mean to take just a sip of wine, but I can't stop. I drain the glass. Luis watches, but in the candlelight his expression is

17

unreadable. He pours my refill in silence. I wait until he's done, until he looks at me again. "I don't do repeats," I tell him.

"I made a mistake."

"Just one?"

He grins, but there's no arrogance in it now. "One after another. But here's the thing, Pélagie. Every one of those mistakes – and they go back all the way to law school, maybe even before – they brought me here. To you, to Al." He reaches across the table, his open hand asking me for – for what? Forgiveness? Acceptance?

I ignore it. "No cheesiness. Please. It's the ultimate insult."

He nods, turns his hand palm down on the table, but leaves it there, invading my space. "I don't want a do-over. I wouldn't take it, except maybe on leaving Al. And I'd do it for him, not for me. These mistakes have been my saving grace. I need you to see it that way, too."

I sit back, as far away from that hand as I can without leaving the table. "How long are you going to do this? Play at this hippie fuck-the-corporate-world shit?"

"I don't know. I –"

"Will you go back to being a lawyer?"

"I don't –"

"Will you stay in Curaçao? In that rented Montaña shack? Will you buy a house?"

"I don't know." He holds my gaze, and I see discomfort. Finally.

"What will happen to Al when you get tired of diving, the way you got tired of lawyering?"

"Wherever I go, he goes. China, Timbuktu –"

"What if you get tired of him, too?"

His eyes darken with anger. "What I got tired of was playing a game where every win is a flash in the pan, nothing's enough, ever. I got tired of living by a measuring stick of achievements that mean nothing except to a tiny group of people. I got tired of working my ass off so some rich dudes could cheat their government."

"Oh, I see. And teaching those same rich dudes to dive is so much loftier?"

He finally pulls his hand back to his side of the table. "I didn't leave, Pélagie. I didn't leave Al, and I didn't leave you."

"This was never about me."

"Then why can't you forgive me?"

I hold my wine glass aloft in a toast. "I can, and I have. What I can't do is trust you."

"Because I don't know where I'll be next year, next month?"

"Because you can't be trusted! Because I'm not a dog. Because, hard as I try, I can't live just in the moment. The future exists, it's coming, and I don't want to get chewed up and spit out."

"You were the one who said no one has a lease on the future. Promises are the worst kind of fallacy, remember? Isn't that what you said?"

I need something to swallow, but my glass is dry. Again. Luis beats me to the bottle. His fingers graze mine as he picks it up.

"Come with me to Bonaire next weekend," he says as he pours.

"No."

His eyes stay on the flow of red. "I'll be diving most of the time, even at night, so you won't have to see me much. Maybe just at breakfast. If you're up early enough."

"No."

"The diving people are great. You'll love them."

"I probably know them already."

He slides the glass, a perfect third full, towards me. "Maybe not. Maybe I can still surprise you. And maybe, if you want, we can stay one more day. Just the two of us. I'm off on Mondays."

He's searching my face with that naive moxie of his.

I take the coward's way out. "I'll think about it," I say.

A lazy afternoon in Bonaire, hammocks, Luis asking me to teach him more ridiculous Dutch expressions. *Now the monkey comes out of the sleeve. They're talking about little cows and little calves.*

Things never go back to the way they were. And perhaps it's for the best. We've no business, none of us, trying to return to the places we were once happy in. All we'll find is blighted hope.

Perhaps all we can do is build anew.

La Ronde / Frank and Madge
by Townsend Walker

Tuesday, 2nd December 2014

A month has passed since Frank figured out Madge had a price on his head and not one of those days has passed without him thinking about how to do her in first. It had to be tight: he knew, no—doubt—about—it, she'd told her friend Gina—the—bitch about how he'd slap her from time to time. Not that Madge didn't deserve it, but it wouldn't look good if they also suspected him of her death. He pretty much had it figured out, but then Thanksgiving rolled around and there was the traditional feast at his family's place upstate near Rhinebeck. He'd do that, but he was damned if he'd go through another Christmas and New Year with her, especially since it was her family's turn this year and her sister Ann was having folks out to their place in Queens. *Queens, for god's sake.* And Ann's husband, what's—his—name, short weasely guy, always wanting inside tips, not understanding (for how many years now) that he was the last person he'd tell. Frank could see it. What's—his—name would make money off the tip, then buy the house rounds. *Got this brother—in—law, horse's mouth, inside scoop.* Sayonara career.

Frank had picked up an old Dell laptop on the street corner the week after seeing Alexei and started to do a bit of research on poison. He tossed the laptop in a dumpster two weeks later.

21

Settled on thallium salts for his conniving Madge. No taste, no color, no smell, no change in food texture, and a tenth of an ounce does the job. His problem: how to get hold of it. Not commercially available. But. As part of his due diligence on the Time Warner/Comcast merger deal he had visited fiber optics manufacturers. (Frank was nothing if not thorough.) The guy who took him through the Corning plant in Wilmington, NC was also named Frank. They hit it off: names and shades (both wore them all the time). Wall Street Frank was Frank the Tall; fiber optic Frank became Frank the Short; FT and FS to each other. After the tour, they had drinks at the City Limits Saloon down by the river and FS told FT about how they used thallium salts to make fiber optic cable. *And we keep that stuff in a special place, toxic as shit; remember that alcove off to the side on the main floor?*

After Thanksgiving FT called FS and said he needed to check a couple more details, flew down, while making the tour: excused himself, dipped into the alcove, grabbed a vial of thallium salt, pocketed it. FT took FS to dinner at Aubriana's downtown where for the third time FS told him how the thallium worked *like a dopant in the lenses, prims and windows of repeaters to speed the signals on their way.* FT nodded politely and moved the conversation to basketball. That carried them into the night: FT was a Buckeye; FS, a Tar Heel. And nearly on to the next morning when FT had to catch his flight.

He came home early today. He knew Madge was meeting Gina for lunch and drinks, and if past history could be depended on, she'd roll in about seven or so. For dinner, he decided to prepare his specialty, Julia Child's stew a la façon de Frank Cabot. Years ago, he discovered he could substitute lamb in her bœuf bourguignon recipe. He assembled the bacon, olive oil, cubed lamb, carrot, onion, red wine, beef stock, cloves, thyme, bay leaf, white wine, butter. He was sautéing the lamb in the hot oil and bacon fat when the kids came home from school, got a car for them to go over to be with Alexei, Sally and their kids for a Hanukkah ceremony (arranged last week). *Even if they're not Jewish, they ought to know about it if they're going to live in this city.*

"Listen up you two, you're going to be doing something different tonight. I want you to be very respectful of what they do and how they do it. Their tradition goes back thousands of years."

"Do we have to eat everything?"

"Take a small bite first. If you don't like it, leave it on the side of the plate. Oh, bring back a potato latke for me, okay."

"Bye Daddy."

Frank adds in the other ingredients, slides the casserole into the oven, pours himself a glass of '07 Cote du Nuit, puts on the CD of Donizetti's *Lucrezia Borgia* (soon to be his favorite), and waits.

Madge clambers through the door, shopping bags akimbo, smelling the stew.

"What a lovely surprise." She drops her bags in the entry and saunters over to him in the chair, leans down and kisses him warmly.

"I thought I'd make us a grown−ups dinner since the kids are out. It will be ready in half an hour."

"I'm famished. I only had a salad for lunch."

"Martini?"

"Why not? Sure."

"How's Gina?"

"Fine. Why? You never ask about her."

"Just wondering."

Madge has a puzzled expression on her face; him asking about her?

"Here's your drink. Cheers to us!"

"Huh?"

23

"To us." He lifts his glass with a flourish.

She slowly brings her glass up to clink his, her expression now one of curiosity.

"Bonus time in a month. Should be a big year."

"What you going to do with it?"

"Buy a boat, maybe, an ocean racer. I sailed as a kid, haven't much since I got out of college. Thought I'd teach Molly and Lance. They had fun last time we were out on Dad's."

"Isn't that kind of dangerous? People fall off. Storms come up out of nowhere, especially these days."

"Things do happen when people aren't careful ... I think it's ready. Sit down."

He brings the vichyssoise (from Gristedes) out from the kitchen.

"Nice, just the right amount of salt." Madge spoons her soup. "I heard this story last summer about a guy sailing with his wife, claimed when he changed course she didn't hear the command, wife was hit by the boom, knocked overboard, he tried but couldn't rescue her."

"The moral is?"

"I don't know if I'd feel safe."

"Aren't you going to finish your vichyssoise?"

"It's feeling heavy in me, not agreeing with something."

"Well, if anything was going to happen, it wouldn't be like that, with the kids around."

Frank excuses himself to serve up the stew.

"What would it be?"

"Something more domestic, probably something slow and painful."

"Did making the stew make you so grim?"

"Hey, you're the one brought up the wife—killing story."

Madge takes a bite of the lamb stew. Frank sits back, as if waiting for her to enjoy. She spits out a mouthful. Chunks land in the middle of the table.

"What the hell did you put in this stew?"

Frank goes down the list of ingredients.

"And what bottle of white wine did you use?"

"It was that half bottle of Chablis left over from last week."

"That was ouzo, you dolt, left over from that Greek meal. Couldn't you smell the difference when it was cooking?"

What a royal screw−up this is. Shit. I cannot believe how fucked up this is. Dammit. He manages the semblance of a straight, please−forgive−me face.

"Hey, it's okay. I'm not gonna die over ouzo−ed lamb."

"How about I go around the corner and pick up some samosas? You like that?"

"And I'll open some real white wine."

Frank grabs his coat, takes the elevator down, thinking *still have enough for another try*, says "How ya keepin', Sammy," to the doorman, turns right, walks about fifty feet, sees a woman: young, tall, long blond hair, high heeled black boots, big coat. Her hands are tucked into her pockets. As she approaches, he moves to his left, she moves to his left, he moves right, she moves right, she comes face to face, eighteen inches apart, icy blue eyes.

"You Frank Cabot?"

"That's me, how'd you …"

She pulls a compact black gun from her pocket. She fires three shots into his heart.

Farewell to Loved Ones
by Derek Osborne

Wednesday, 3rd December 2014

"**N**o Eddie, I will be fine," Rebecca says, "I just need this time to be alone."

Eddie closes the cabin door. Rebecca can hear him walking back down the passageway. It is freezing cold aboard *Gadabout* but she does not feel it; she is wearing the foul weather gear Max had specially made for her, the brown knit cap they bought that day on Martha's Vineyard, the silk t—shirt her mother insisted upon.

The cabin is just how they left it, the bunk made up with the patchwork quilt, the pillows piled high along the bulkhead. All the fittings have been polished bright, the mahogany and painted white millwork detailed to perfection. The desk and the drawers – the drawers – she fumbles with the thing inside her pocket. Rebecca is here to complete the contract. They have a buyer. *Gadabout* will have a new captain. Tradition dictates the owner's drawer must hold the one thing he could not do without, the one thing they cannot let go. It weighs there in the cargo fold of her jacket. As Max's wife, it is Rebecca who now owns *Gadabout*, Rebecca who will sign the papers. The nights they spent together drift through the cabin. The gray winter day shows through the skylight. Rebecca stands as if on an empty stage, the performance done, the echo of a standing ovation drifting across the proscenium.

"I hear you, my love. I hear you."

The wind pushes the hull. It snowed a bit this morning, only a dusting, but enough to cause her mother to make a fuss about her coming out to the boat.

"So now your baby will be motherless as well."

"And you call me the drama queen."

"I'm afraid you inherited your father's common sense."

"Do not go there, Mama. You married him for it. And I know you loved that in Max. Do not tell me otherwise."

This made her mother grow quiet.

Rebecca is taking in every detail, every moment – their love–making, their fights, the quiet times; their talk that last evening – their pact. Baby Max, though premature, is the picture of health. He has his father's hair, his mother's lungs. Andi enjoys calling him little brother.

Rebecca can feel the wind outside. The mizzen creaks in the mast step, another gust. *Gadabout* swings to face it. She scans the ship's library, all the books she intended to read, all those evenings curled up together snug and warm and sailing the great, wide ocean. This cabin was to be home, a sense of generations, more than anywhere else on the boat the place of so many lives completed, the empty chair at the desk, the mirror hanging over the sink. She looks at the drawers again. The fifth drawer, what was to be Max's drawer only, now hers as well. Max never said what to put in it. He never discussed it with Eddie. Eddie could not, or would not, help. She feels again the thing in her pocket. She hopes it is the right choice.

"Is it, my darling? Did I know you that well?"

Eleven months, a lifetime in eleven months. Touching the drawer is not easy. Pulling it open even harder. Like peering down into an empty grave. The wind will not back down. Outside the light has turned leaden and gray.

"The sun for all its sorrow ..."

The bearers are coming, the graves men stand to one side. Rebecca takes the SAT phone from inside her jacket, its weathered red case and black stub of antenna strange in her hand. The weight of it, heavy and solid. She folds the antenna into its little niche, pressing the instrument down between the sides of the drawer. Her hand is shaking. She cannot bring herself to close it, not yet.

"Are you here with me, Max? Am I the good shepherd?"

Gadabout shifts again. Rebecca leans back against the bunk.

"I had no idea what would come of a single kiss. Driving home that night from the restaurant. Sitting in your lap. I only knew I had found you – again – after all this time."

She takes one last look around the cabin.

"And now you are gone, and now we will have to find each other again."

Reaching back, she pulls the patchwork quilt off the bunk. She promised the girls she would bring it. Folding it over and over, clutching the worn and bulky softness to her face, his scent fills her eyes, his warmth flows inside her. She knows it is time to leave. If she does not leave now Eddie will have to carry her. The open drawer awaits the final rose, the fist–full of dirt, the turn and walk from the pastor's stranger's smile. The SAT phone's screen is blank, lifeless. Max once told her the sound of it coming alive was the sweetest thing he has ever known. She reaches into the drawer, pushing the big red button. The backlight warms, searching for satellites. STANDBY appears in the upper right corner. Gently, she pushes the little drawer closed. Go now, the boat whispers. At the cabin door she waits before turning the latch – not hoping it will ring; knowing it will not ring, but giving it time nonetheless – giving Gadabout the chance at one more miracle. Who better than Rebecca to know such things only happen in the movies, and after all, she was only a cable TV star, and even then, only a little while. All will move on, now. All will move on.

Chanukah
by Gloria Garfunkel

Thursday, 4th December 2014

Bipolar Ralph here. It's a month since my father's death / suicide. My father always loved Chanukah the best of Jewish holidays because it was totally joyous despite the Destruction of the Temple in Jerusalem. He loved the miracle of one candle in oil lasting eight nights and the renewal of the Temple. He always bought everyone presents, me, my five siblings and their kids. Manic toys on all eight days.

My father's gift theory for kids was quantity over quality. It didn't matter if it broke the next day, just get them a lot of things.

I decide to take over his job and do the same thing. I have plenty of time to spy on what everyone wants, all ten nieces and nephews. Chanukah is eight days starting Thursday the 16th. I think about Chloe. She's the best thing in my life. I'm just numb for now, for a moment, though I know I'm on my way to euphoric, but for now content and calm. A blessing. I'm probably due for some mania around New Year's. It always precedes a depression. I can see what Chloe's father's suicide has done to her. I could never hurt her like that again.

There's a Jewish custom on Rosh Hashanah to go to a river and throw away your sins in crumbs of bread. I drive out to the river and throw in all my suicide paraphernalia so it's never a temptation: my gun, my years of hoarded pills, my noose, the knives, razor blades, and the thick plastic bag for over my head. I swear my bipolar will never kill me or my kids.

We'll do our best like everyone else. Who cares some say bipolars shouldn't have kids? We'll educate them early about the illness. We'll medicate them. I'm buying the ring I picked out and I'm going to ask Chloe to marry me tomorrow.

Ivory
by John Wentworth Chapin

Friday, 5th December 2014

A tote of cleaning supplies rests on the kitchen counter above a messy bundle of coat hangers and an over–filled trash can. White rectangles pop from the walls, nuclear shadows of dethroned artwork outlined by dirt and grease. Everything he's taking with him is in his car.

"You need a therapist," Stephanie drones through the invisible speaker of Charles' phone.

"No, I need a philosopher," he answers. Moving is usually a terrible chore, but not this move.

Charles' terrible watercolor portrait of Esther sits propped against the wall by the door. He took it from his closet and put it in the *garbage* pile, then moved it to the *keep–it* pile, then tossed it to the *donations* pile, then pulled it back out. Now it's in limbo. He puts it back in the *garbage* pile.

Stephanie's voice is thin, powerless. "What if you move and it doesn't solve anything, but now you're unemployed and alone?"

"I'm not moving," he reminds her. "I'm leaving. I will be traveling, and when I stop, I expect to end up in a different place."

On the kitchen counter, atop a mound of desk debris, lies his little memory book. Charles picks up the book and flips through it while Stephanie monologues. So many things dear to him are jotted inside. He writes down important events and then looks back to celebrate. So he is always looking back.

Stephanie continues. "I don't think it's particularly healthy to slam the door closed on your life."

"I look backwards too much, don't I?" he says.

Silence. Then: "Are you even listening to me?" Stephanie asks.

Charles isn't listening to her. He's staring at the page for today, December 5. He sees the note for today, carefully drawn with a box around it and three stars, which in his important−events rating system is a Top Event.

"Charles?"

"Holy shit," he murmurs.

"If this is a ploy for attention, it's working," she says.

"Today's the one−year anniversary of the accident."

"Are you okay?" Stephanie asks.

"I'm fine," he says. But he's alarmed that he didn't realize until now what today is: a momentous day.

The evening waterfront is dark and cold and desolate except for a few joggers, women with strollers, women jogging with strollers. It's quiet down here, only distant traffic breaking over the murmur of water lapping the pilings. Charles ambles along the harbor's edge, saying goodbye. Fell's Point is his favorite − or was his favorite − place to walk with Stephanie, an unbroken stretch of the water's edge meandering around the ritzy condos and highrises that replaced the dilapidated maritime mess of his childhood. *Maybe I'll come back. Eventually.*

A stroller rolls across in front of him, so fast it almost hits him. Then it careens into the harbor.

Charles spins, but there's no one around. He looks over the edge to see the spot where the stroller floats on its side in the black, trash—speckled water. He's certain enough that there's a baby in the stroller that he jumps in next to it; the water rushes up cold and black and he can see nothing, but he feels something pushing against his leg and he grabs: a length of metal. He then catches something squishy, an arm or leg. He tries to pull it up to his chest. Kicking with all his might, he manages to hoist it out of the water.

He's holding the metal side of the stroller and a small foot swaddled in what feels like a wet pot—holder. Charles tries to lift the baby out of the stroller, but it is strapped in. He puts both hands underneath to lift baby and stroller out of the water together. It's nearly impossible to keep the baby's face and his own mouth out of the water. The baby issues a blood—curdling scream; Charles kicks to keep himself upright while he fumbles for a clip or buckle to get the baby out. Then he hears a woman's voice and a splash and more hands reaching for the baby. Charles shouts for the person to grab the stroller and keep it up. He puts his hands under the baby's armpits and then pulls it up, now free of the stroller. He sets the baby on his chest and kicks backwards toward the bulkhead wall. The baby alternates shrieks and deep gasps for air.

It's cold, and the weight of the water in his shoes, in the baby's clothes, is beginning to wear Charles down. The young woman asks if her baby boy is all right. Charles says he is but they need to get out of the water quickly, and he works his way along the bulkhead until he feels the cross—bars of a ladder. The mother splashes along behind Charles cooing to her son between sputters of fear and grief.

When they've clambered out of the water, the woman takes the baby from him, wrapping her body around it. She's sobbing, and the baby is screaming. Charles reaches for his iPhone to call 911, but of course when he hits a button, it's dead, waterlogged.

He flags down help and a small crowd gathers.

"He saved my baby!" the woman shouts. A man in the crowd removes his sweatshirt for the baby, and now it's swaddled in a cream—colored hoodie. When Charles hears sirens approaching, he quietly slips away from the crowd, wet shoes sloshing beneath him on the cobblestones.

"I'm looking for Chuck," Charles says. He's soaking wet, but he has one more goodbye, so he's back at Eastern Antiques for the last time.

Deonna stands in the back doorway with her arms crossed and a sour look on her face. "If you find him, tell the cops. They're looking for him, too."

She could be bluffing, either trying to scare Charles or keep him away from Chuck. Then again: *Chuck.*

"Holy fuck! You're dripping all over my floor! Get out."

"I rescued a baby from the harbor."

"Jesus. Sure you did. Time to hang a youie and go back to rehab."

"I never stole anything from you," Charles says. "Do you have a phone number for him? My phone is … messed up."

"Just get out. Don't come back or I'm calling the cops," Deonna replies, jabbing at the air with her finger.

"You're awfully quick to call the cops for a drug smuggler," Charles said.

Deonna says, "I'm telling you, take a hike or you'll be sorry."

He picks up the phone next to the register. "9—1—1. They're required to come, even if I hang up. Maybe you don't have any drugs in the shop. Maybe you do. But you'll be on their radar —"

"Put down that phone," Deonna says. "I got a pistol in my office."

"And if I know you, it's probably not properly registered," Charles answers. He knows better than to take his eyes off her. "You fucked my asshole father, and he stole from you. Threaten me all you want, but nothing changes that. Just give me his phone number."

She scowls at him, thinking, then leans back into her office. Charles steels himself, but she turns back around holding her iPhone. It's swathed in an oversized, pink and purple, jewel−encrusted bumper that stretches around the edge of the phone for protection. Deonna peers closely at it, makes a few swipes, and then lays it on the counter by the register, her recent call list with CHUCK and several other numbers facing him.

Charles has a glorious moment of clarity.

He asks Deonna for a piece of paper, and while she turns back to the office, he pops her phone out of its bumper and replaces it with his own destroyed phone. His is black and hers is white, and he can only hope she doesn't notice. He slips her phone into his pocket. When she returns with paper, he writes random numbers quickly.

"Thanks," he mumbles.

"Tell him to fuck himself. And don't you come back, neither," Deonna shouts after him.

Once outside, he quickly retrieves Deonna's phone to make sure it's still unlocked; it is.

Hallelujah! With her unlocked phone, Charles has carte blanche to wreak havoc. He calls the police from Deonna's own phone to make an anonymous tip about some hash smuggling.

He giggles as he texts his father on Deonna's behalf, begging for a couple of cocktails and one last hot screw. If all goes well, Chuck will show up at the shop. He emails himself Chuck's contact information for future reference. He can unload all the old Chuck debt once he knows where to find him.

Charles forwards himself a few incriminating emails between Deonna and her shipper in Vietnam. When he gets around to it, he'll forward them on to U.S. Customs. With such lovely technology, it doesn't take him long to do a lot of damage.

He calls his mother and tells her he's leaving; she insists on saying goodbye in person, despite his objections. He sighs and agrees to meet her back at his apartment. Instead of ending the call, he tosses Deonna's phone into the harbor.

Ah, revenge. Esther would approve.

The walls, the floor, the doors: everything shabby, dingy white. His mother stands with her arms crossed in his kitchen, radiating disapproval and Shalimar.

"Why do you have to leave tonight? Why would you start such a big trip at *night*?"

She doesn't want to hear his answer, so there's no point explaining. "I rescued a baby from the harbor," Charles said.

She furrows her brows. "When?"

"Just this evening. I was walking and a stroller zoomed by with a baby in it and rolled into the harbor in Fell's. I saved its life." A year ago, carnage. Now this.

"I'm very concerned about you, Charles," she says. She clearly doesn't believe him; Charles doesn't quite believe himself.

"That's probably wise," he answers. He indicates the door that he wants her to depart through. Charles' mother walks stiffly out into the hall.

Charles takes a final look around. He leaves the key on the kitchen counter and spots the memory book, lying there undecided. Charles lobs it atop the *garbage* pile on the floor, where it knocks into the watercolor canvas. Charles stoops to collect his painting and walks off into an opaque future, the portrait of Esther tucked securely under his arm.

Fleeting
by Lynn Beighley

Saturday, 6th December 2014

"**Y**ou're her, aren't you? That one from that reality show, *You Tell Me?*"

I turn from the rack of blouses to see a skinny, overly made up sales girl smiling at me.

"You are! Oh. My. God. This is so cool! Look, can we take a selfie? No one will believe this."

I shrug. Maybe I'll get a discount on the clothes I need to buy for my new cubicle job. I could use it.

She stands next to me, puts her arm over my shoulder and cheek next to mine, and we smile as though we are best friends having the best time ever. Best. Ever. The.

Photo shoot done, she glances around. Seeing no one but me watching, she taps on the screen sending the proof of our giddiness out to all the sites where such things go today. Done, she turns back to me.

"God, thank you soooooo much!" She glances at the clothes draped over my arm. "Oh, let me get you a fitting room. Those are going to look soooo great on you. I just adore your red hair." She's beaming at me. I nod and she takes my clothes and sets me up with a dressing room.

I let her help me find some more clothes. She seems thrilled to help me look good, and I'm happy to let her. I'm optimistic

37

that a discount will happen.

I'm trying on a blue shirt that she swears will bring out my eyes (taken literally, that's an alarming image), when she laughs.

"My boyfriend wants to know ..." she pauses. "He's asking about Bill Plover's nickname. He wants to know." She's giggling so much she has trouble talking. "Okay, so on the honeymoon, was he Bill Dozer because he slept a lot? Or Bill Dozer because he was, um, unstoppable?"

Shit. She thinks I'm April, the Jessica Rabbit–looking woman he married last month. She doesn't realize I'm the evil redheaded woman who turned him down. Crap.

I take a deep breath. I really want that discount. Okay. I can do this.

"Ha ha," I pretend laugh. "Both. Tell your boyfriend it was both."

I try on a few more outfits, and with the help of my new best friend, end up with a nice work wardrobe. I let her think I'm the newlywed. And it pays off, I do get a nice discount. She wraps my clothes in tissue, as she chatters on about the show and how it changed her life and how she wishes she could be on a show like it and how she's applied for a bunch of them and they never call her back and how she's put some of her business cards in my shopping bag in case I hear of any shows that might be looking for someone like her, someone with some acting experience (she was the lead in tons of plays in high school and just loves acting) and she hopes we can go out to lunch some time (when Bill has let me get enough rest, heh heh) and talk it all over.

I smile graciously and nod, and say yes, of course, and you'd be perfect. I take my bag of work clothes and drape it over my shoulder and leave the store. I walk out to my beat–up yellow car, and shove the bag in the bag seat.

My phone rings. I see it's a Los Angeles area code. I listen to it ring three times. My finger almost presses the mute button, but instead I tap the Answer button.

"Season two of *You Tell Me*, Jenn. We want you."

Ant

by Andrew Stancek

Sunday, 7th December 2014

The body is leeched of colour. The creases around the eyes and nose have smoothed; the mouth is freed of the howls.

The monitor blips brain activity but the chest does not rise and fall.

Antiseptic silence. A pale blue vase on the night table holds wilted remnants of a white sweet pea, edges curled.

An eyelid twitches. The darkness outside breaks with a ray of light. A chirp. A rustle of wings.

From a corner of the room a six−legged wingless ant, indistinguishable from billions of its brothers, marches three steps and stops. It lifts into the air, circles, circles, circles. The human body shudders and the monitor flatlines.

The ant soars through the crack in the open window, towards the sun, and disappears.

It is only the beginning.

Christmas Fettucine
by Rachel Ambrose

Monday, 8th December 2014

"It's coming on Christmas, they're cuttin' down trees
..." The melancholy lyrics of Joni Mitchell's 'River'
wend their languorous, sad way out of my sister
Molly's speakers. We've decided to have a classic tree—trimming
party complete with English crackers (which explode), American
crackers (which hopefully do not), and altogether too much
mulled wine for a Monday evening. But Molly's longtime
girlfriend has just walked out on her. Sometimes an older sister
needs a younger sister to watch *Miracle on 34th Street* with her
and feed her inordinate amounts of alcohol to help her get over
life's setbacks. I've taken the liberty of inviting Isa, because we
cannot be expected to subsist only on Triscuits and cheap booze.

"Do you have any tinsel?" I ask Molly as we unearth the last
of the ornaments from the dust—covered Christmas Box. "Or
stale popcorn?"

"I think there might be some up in the attic, in the New
Year's box," she replies. "I moved it somewhere last year after
we pulled it out for a party ... Michelle wore it like a feather boa
..." Her eyes well and she presses a crumpled tissue to her face.

I hug her. "Please forget about that loser, okay? You'll be
fine. You can't possibly be less successful than me, and I've

become pretty darn successful this past year. The world just wouldn't stay on its axis. You're a lawyer, for goodness sake."

It's true: my gallery job is still going well (although I have given up forever on trying to figure out what Frederico does with those four−hour time gaps; I figure it's one of the great mysteries of the universe, and that I'm somehow better off not knowing). Diogenes is still creaking away and leaving fur trails all over the apartment, and I've managed to find myself still single and, rather miraculously, not hating every second of it. I've become a voracious reader in my spare time and have even started to hand in little blurbs about the books I read to the local paper.

The fake tree is almost toppling with our childhood ornaments, which Molly insisted on taking for herself when we were going through our parents' attic. She thought she would keep them for when she and Michelle got married and had kids of their own. Clearly that's not happening now. I wonder briefly if I might be able to steal a few. I'd forgotten how cute our youthful efforts at arts and crafts were. So many Popsicle sticks. So much glue peeking around the edges of ancient glittered macaroni.

"Pre−Christmas fettucine is almost ready," says Isa from her perch at the stove. "Where do you guys keep your bowls?"

I dig out the good bone−china bowls from Molly's sideboard and swipe a few forks from the dish drain as Isa pours us more red wine from the bottle on the counter. "You know," she says as she peppers the pasta, "it hasn't been a half−bad year."

I raise a glass at her as Molly comes back into the kitchen, draped with enough tinsel to make a drag queen cry. "It ain't over yet, sweetheart," I say, taking a gulp and squeezing Molly's shoulder as she passes me on her way to the tree. "There's still just enough time for a dance party."

Realationships and rules
by Gill Hoffs

Tuesday, 9th December 2014

I'm meant to be seeing Trudi at the salon today for some festive fanny-hair, probably a Christmas tree or a snowflake, but instead of a wax I'm sat in Zoe's chair in the office, spinning round while she nips for a wee or worse and I cover the (thankfully silent) phone. We'd been discussing the best manicure for a work-wank, which finishes would survive a strum, whether glued-on crystals can come off, and the horrors of acrylics and nail piercings, so perhaps it's just all the mental images of yours truly getting her hot under her hemline.

Though her vibrator's still in her stash drawer, nestled beside the emergency Maltesers and Tampax, so perhaps not.

Wondering whether a snowflake's sexiest, I type '2318008' on her calculator and as I turn it upside down to check I spelled 'boobies' right, the phone rings. I learnt my answering voice from *Madmen.*

"Good morning, might I ask what services you require?"

And it's him. Rory.

"Hello, yes, good morning. Is it still morning? Feels like afternoon but I've been up ages."

There's a bit of a quiver in his voice, and he's rambling – nervous? Could he be nervous? – but it's definitely him.

"Indeed, sir. And how are you today?"

I've spent enough time chilling out here with Zoe, eavesdropping while she takes bookings and doles out assignments and flirts, to know her standard lines and repeat the script word for word. Just as well. My cheeks are burning and I doubt I'd string a sentence together otherwise.

"Fine, fine. Bit busy but fine. I was wondering if you still had a certain girl working for you – I, um, spent some time with her in March."

I swallow what feels like a pint of saliva that's suddenly swilling about my mouth and hope to goodness Zoe's got a magazine in the loo with her. Something with an article on Will and Kate and babies and whether every parent should have their own version of Lupo blah blah blah. Something to get her daydreaming about princes, princesses, and dogs the colour of my (over)cooking.

"Can you be more specific? I can certainly check that for you."

I can hear him gulp, but no sip or slurp beforehand. *Is* he nervous too?

"She's beautiful." He coughs out a little laugh. "Sorry, that hardly narrows it down, does it? Um, she had long dark hair, freckles on the bridge of her nose, green eyes, and a slight Manchester accent. She went by Jennifer."

No mention of my boobs or my fabulous arse? Fuckssake.

"Jennifer … yes, I know who you mean. Would you like me to arrange another meeting with her? Do you have a particular date in mind?"

Whenever it is, I'm free. Even if I have to plead food poisoning to Zoe and whoever I'm already booked with to make it.

"Tonight, if she's available." Yes! "Or any evening this week. I can be flexible." Him and me both. I click at Zoe's keyboard with my sex−safe French manicure, typing his name and mine for the sake of a sound effect and making Zoe's screensaver of the bald guy from *Masterchef* holding an enormous cucumber vanish, revealing a spreadsheet of things going in and out in more ways than one.

"She's free tonight. Where and when should she meet you?"

"If she can be ready for collection at six from wherever is most convenient for her to be picked up then that would be great."

Six! I don't know if I can wait.

"Certainly. Is this for a special occasion or setting? Will you be emailing any information for her to read or any particular requirements?"

I wonder what he works as. Vet? Scientist? Surgeon? Something caring, anyway. I wonder if this a business date?

"No, no, nothing like that. I was hoping to take her for dinner in Sheffield then, if she cares to, to a spa for the night."

Oh!

"Should I check her schedule for tomorrow?"

"Yes, of course. Sorry, yes. Actually, could you check it for the next couple of days while you're at it?"

Hmm ... I know I've a Christmas business do to go to on Thursday but the client's only requested a slim brunette in her 20's so I can always swap with Sophie or Kim if I need to.

"Her schedule is free or flexible through to Saturday. Shall I suggest to her an overnight case?"

"No, no, I can buy her whatever she needs. Unless you think she might prefer her own things?"

Dammit, I can hear a toilet flushing.

"I'll mention the situation to her, sir. She'll be waiting for you at the agency at six."

"Great, great. Thank you."

I'm clapping my hands and spinning on Zoe's chair, full circle, full speed, when she returns from the loo muttering about Harry and the Queen.

"What's *that* smile for?" she asks, staying well out of range.

"I've ... got ... a ... *date*!"

Trudi sorted me out as best she could. I definitely did *not* want to look like I'd slipped a freshly plucked chicken breast in my knickers but equally I'd no intention of turning up for this date with spider–legs creeping down my thighs. It's amazing what a woman with tweezers and strong glasses can do.

After two hours of rejecting outfits, emptying my wardrobe, and shooing my cat off the piles of clothing on my bed, I'd decided on a pale jade sweater with a deep v–neck to show off the pearl pendant Rory gave me at his ex's wedding nine months ago. Nine whole months. Enough to grow a baby, perhaps someday a mini–me. It shows off my cleavage a little too, but not overtly, and the skirt is a rich purply velvet swirl around my knees. The boots are black suede, comfortable but sexy, my makeup subtle and a little bit student–y, with a smudge of lilac glitter sparkling round my eyes. No perfumes or scented lotions. I feel jittery but confident, or so I tell myself.

And unlike any other work–night, I'm dressed as me.

Zoe keeps looking at me from behind her desk, I can see her reflection in the glass as I peer out the window at the busy street below. I don't know what he drives but it seems a waste to miss a moment of him, so I watch it all.

"New look for you tonight. Suits you."

I don't turn round but I do meet her eyes in the glass and wink. It's like she is actually seeing me, *me* not Jennifer.

"Thanks, Zoe."

She opens her mouth to say something else but the phone on the desk rings the abbreviated *brrring* that warns her someone's approaching our door and I nearly giggle or sing.

The door opens and he's here and gorgeous.

He nods a quick hello to Zoe then his deep–denim eyes fix on me. There are about five million hair follicles on the average human body, and every single one of mine seems to be vibrating like a happy bee.

"Hi ..." He steps closer and smells of sandalwood incense.

"Hi ... great to see you again." *I'm−a−fool−I'm−a−fool−say−something−BETTER* runs through my head. I need to make sure this is what I hope it is. "Are we meeting colleagues or family tonight ...?"

He shakes his head, and I love how his smile crinkles his face and moves his freckles into fresh constellations on his cheeks.

"Would Italian suit you tonight, Jennifer?"

I blush and grin, my cheeks like tomatoes.

"I'm Carla, Carla Donovan." I hear Zoe gasp at my breaking house rules but I really don't care. "Anything's fine with me."

Oranges
by Susan Tepper

Wednesday, 10th December 2014

"When your mind is made up, it's made up," Pedersen tells the white rat. Swoon, on the arm of the chair, nibbles Frito crumbs out of Pedersen's palm. "If you were a man I'd expect you to understand. But you're not. You're a third-world rodent. That white fur won't save your ass."

Pedersen rests his head back. The Barcalounger, from the year of the flood, has the same type of headrest as a dentist chair. "What a piece of shit," he says, dusting his hands together. The white rat, Swoon, flees.

"Good-bye," he tells it.

Frankly, he'll be glad to be rid of it. The rat has become a nuisance. It used to appear occasionally, when it smelled cooking, or when there was take-out food in a bag on the table. Lately it comes out of its rat hole whenever he's home. Even when he'd rather be alone with his thoughts. His mind drifting now to warm skies with sunshine bearing down and palm trees along the roadsides. Not this slushy sludge of winter. Winter being the worst time of the year. Winter they keep the kiddies locked in the school, no coming out for recess. God forbid they should catch a sniffle. His little darlings.

Florida will be a nice change of pace. Down there it will be warm most of the time and the kiddies will be everywhere. They'll be bright in their little kiddie clothes and flying around like a bunch of colorful kites. Running, screeching, squealing, laughing, shouting. He can park his car outside the schoolyard (per usual) almost the entire year down there.

Pedersen's knees creak when he gets out of the Barcalounger. Good oranges down there, too.

All the Little Labels
by Jessica McHugh

Thursday, 11th December 2014

Nelson Wade loads a box into the moving van. Falling snow hits his nose, and he rubs the cold spot as he faces Edward McKenzie.

"It's going to be weird without you around, Father."

Edward clamps a pink mitten to Nelson's shoulder. "You don't have to call me that anymore. I'm just plain old Edward now." He flips his blonde wig and bats his eyelashes. "With a touch of flair, of course."

The altar boy laughs, and Edward's heart warms in the frigid December afternoon. After resigning from his position at St. Peter's, and the backlash following his explanation, he's grateful for any kindness offered. Nelson is one of the few who stuck by him when he entered the church garbed in a Sunday dress to rival the most fashionable ladies in the congregation. For the first time, he spoke his confession outside of the confessional and felt no shame, even after those he'd once counseled cast their aspersions. Since his mother's death, Edward McKenzie has refused to hide, refused to be unhappy with his truth.

He assumes he could've loaded the boxes alone, but now that he stands among them, he's glad for the company. Especially when he realizes how many he's marked with 'Eleanor' and 'Betty' instead of 'Edward'. All the boxes, all the little labels.

Each one contains a portion of a life he built from the lives of others, too afraid to live his own.

Not anymore. Fairvale will have its close—minded people, too — he's certain of it — but it'll also have its Nelson Wades. And Mario.

His heart flutters when his boyfriend's face fills his mind. His boyfriend, his boyfriend. He can't stop thinking it. *I have a boyfriend.*

Edward's phone rings, and he digs it out of his coat. Ripping off his mitten, he swipes the screen, presses the phone to his ear, and says, "A whole hour without talking to me. That's a record so far."

Mario chuckles. "I just wanted to let you know I'm leaving the office to come help you now. I'll be there in thirty."

"We're nearly finished. I'll be ready to leave for the new place before you get here."

He sighs. "I'm sorry, babe. I should've been there to help you. I just got hung up at work."

Edward had figured Mario wouldn't be able to make it in time to help him move, but as he's become used to such disappointments, he'd prepared himself for the letdown.

"Really, don't worry about it. It's okay."

A car horn catches Edward's attention. Mario's car pulls to a stop at the curb, and he says, smiling, "It is now."

Edward's grin shines from his entire body as his boyfriend jogs over to embrace him. He twirls his fingers through Edward's golden waves as they kiss. Mario's lips taste of espresso and spearmint, and his breath fills Edward with heat until he no longer feels the snow.

When they break apart, Edward glimpses Nelson's averted eyes.

He blushes. "Sorry, Nelson. You can go on home if you want. Thank you for all the help."

"Glad to do it, Father — whoops, sorry. I know that's not who you are anymore."

Edward squeezes his crucifix with a smile. "Man or woman, I'll always be a child and shepherd of God. I'll always worship and love Him. He made me who I am. He gave me strength and illuminated my path to a better life."

Mario hooks his arm in Edward's. "And brought us together."

Edward can hardly believe his joy. Fear still dwells in his heart, but it feels different from the fear that's haunted most of his life. Instead of terror inspired by his mother's insults and threats, instead of needing the ghost of his Grandma Eleanor to assuage him, instead of believing he has no place in God's heart, he sees hope in not knowing the future. He might not find it in a new church, maybe not even with Mario in the new town, but he believes a happy future lies in his ability to take the first steps on his own.

Edward hugs his former altar boy, his chin quivering as he thanks him again. "God bless you, Nelson. Without you, I might not have had the courage to begin this journey."

Nelson pats his back, grinning. "You would have. It just might've taken another year."

As the altar boy disappears around the corner, Edward wonders if they'll cross paths again. If not, he knows Nelson will grow into a wonderful human being. He is another man's child, another social circle's friend – in theory, he shouldn't have given Edward McKenzie anything but service in the Lord's name, but he gave more than anyone. It's amazing how something as small as acceptance can change a person's life in such colossal ways.

Mario slides the last box into the back of Edward's car, and pulls him into his arms.

"Have I told you how beautiful you look today?" he asks.

Edward blushes and toes the frozen ground. "I look like a big fat bell in this coat."

Shaking his head, Mario links his arms around Edward's back and kisses his nose. "You look like a beautiful woman in the snow. A *princess*. My girlfriend is a princess."

He thought "boyfriend" was a great word, but "girlfriend" sounds even lovelier.

"Princess Edward," he continues. "Hmm ... that doesn't really match your beauty, does it?" Tapping the box labeled 'Eleanor McKenzie' in the back seat, he says, "How about Princess Eleanor?"

He smiles. "No, not Eleanor."

"You're going to need a new name sometime, don't you think?"

Gazing into his boyfriend's eyes, he says, "Yes. And when I pick one, you'll be the first to know."

High and Bye
by Shane Simmons

Friday, 12th December 2014

"You did what?!" I ask. I'm standing in the doorway, an empty cardboard box in my arms.

Sandra sits there, one hand grasping the obligatory glass of wine, her other arm wrapped up in a sling.

"You heard me," she says. "I climbed out of the window."

I walk into the room and pause to look her in the eye, just to see if she's bullshitting me.

She's not.

Shaking my head, I continue to the corner where I sit on the floor and start lifting handfuls of books from the bottom shelf, into the box. "I've said it before and I'll say it again. You are absolutely fucking barmy."

"I don't know what I was thinking."

I shake my head again.

"That waste of space was more upset about his Xbox smashing to pieces when I threw it out of the window than when I was threatening to jump. But hey, whatever. I've seen this Sherice he was sexting and believe me, I'm his loss."

I want to let her know that from the moment I met Marlon I never saw him as anything but a trussed up little prick. But I'm certain I don't need to. "Then what happened?"

"Well, a few people stopped on the pavement and were watching and some knob even shouted for me to jump! Oh, and someone put a photo on Twitter! Hold on, I favourited it ..." She pops down the wine glass and with her one available hand, rummages through her handbag and pulls out her phone.

"Here!" She turns the screen to me and sure enough there's a blurry shot of her flat and as I lean in closer I see a pair of legs hanging from her window ledge.

"That's just before someone called the police! You won't believe this though, remember that shoplifter, in the shop across the road?"

"Oh yeah, tied back hair, council estate facelift, millions of kids. What's she got to do with this?"

"No! Remember the officer who turned up?"

I shake my head, "No ..."

"Yes you do! I know you do because you were staring at him! You do realise that you do that, don't you?" She leers at me with googly eyes.

"I don't do that! Okay, yes, I remember him. Really tall, amazing eyes, blondish hair?"

"Yeah, well he was one of the officers and when I saw him coming up the path, looking up at my fat, pale dangling legs, well I felt a right tit. So I thought, fuck this, I better get down."

"Hmm ..." I've barely cleared half the shelf and I need another empty box so I spin around on my backside to face her and give her my full attention.

"So while Marlon was kicking off about all the stuff of his I'd chucked out ... his clothes, Calvins ... And maybe his laptop ... and the Xbox ... Anyway, so I swung around to get back in, twisted and turned, and then I made a right arse of it."

I point to her bandaged arm.

She draws out a "Yeeaahh ..." and fixes her eyes on her shoes, embarrassed.

As I pick up one last book to try and cram into the box, I wave my other hand to prompt her to continue.

"Well, I fell into the room from the window sill. And you know how high the windows are in these flats!"

My howl bounces around the room.

"Yes, yes, laugh all you want!"

"Sorry," I say, but my snickers continue.

"I put my arm out to stop myself but it twisted around under me and ended up between my chest and the floor! I've bruised three ribs as well you know!"

"I'd have thought your boobs would've cushioned you."

"Ha−bloody−ha."

I give her the two−fingered salute.

"Anyway ... an ambulance came, they took me to MY hospital! All the girls kept popping by to poke fun at me and then they wouldn't let me out in case I was 'a danger to myself'! Oh, and then they called my mother ..."

"You Sandra, are one prize twonk."

She shrugs her shoulders and winces, touches her sore ribs. "Aren't I just?"

Now we're sitting in a room dotted with chock−full packing boxes. "Here, you finish this." Sandra holds the bottle in my direction. "I've had enough. And stop packing things because you're hardly going anywhere."

She's only a couple of glasses through the bottle and I wonder if she didn't bash her head too during her mock−suicide tumble.

"I've told you Sandra, I am. And I don't have long to pack."

"No, I'm not letting you leave here. You can potter about, putting all your things into these bloody boxes − WHY?! WHY DO YOU HAVE TO GO?!" Her shrill bounces off the walls and the vibrating shakes my eardrums.

I weave around boxes and sit down on the sofa next to her.

"I applied for that job. I didn't get the job. And then, at the last minute, the guy they chose pulled out. And not just that, it's not even the role I applied for, it's management. Nearly double what I'm earning at the moment. I could hardly pass up that opportunity!"

"Nah, it's not that," she shakes her head. "It's because it's Scotland, isn't it? It's that boy? The half–Scottish one? Mark! You think you're going to meet him again, don't you?"

I stand up and navigate around the boxes to the TV stand in the corner of the room, and start picking up DVDs from the floor around it and stacking them one on top of the other.

"That wine has gone straight to your head," I say. "You don't know what you're talking about."

"Oh, but I do. See, I know we're both fuck–ups. You know I can't help but keep attracting these cheating, bastarding wasters and I know you've not *really* let him go as yet, have you?"

I turn around to face her just as the tower of DVDs topples like dominos between the boxes. "Sand, if Mark walked past me right this minute, I probably wouldn't even recognise him, and I'm sure he's all sorted in the romance department by now. And just because he's half–Scottish doesn't mean he's going to turn up in Scotland. The world is a big place, you know."

"I know that, but do you?" Her eyes bore holes straight through mine. And I want her to stop.

"I know, Sandra." I bend down to gather up the scattered DVD boxes around my feet, "I know all too well."

"I think I should come to Scotland for Christmas. It's not that far. Or how about New Year's? We can each find our own cabers to toss! I'm not leaving without your new address!!!"

Picking up the notepad and red pen from the coffee table, she rips my 'to–do' list off the top and stretching across, brandishes the blank sheet and the red pen in my direction.

Dust

by Michelle Elvy

Saturday, 13th December 2014

"That's us," says Ellie at the sound of the boarding call. She takes Stevie's hands and pulls him close.

"Yeah." Stevie laces her fingers in his. "You take care of Manny, right?"

She smiles. "You know I will."

They lean their foreheads together. They are exactly the same height and they close their eyes, noses touching. They inhale and exhale and remain this way for a few long moments, each feeling the other's breath, warm and familiar. He will not feel her breath on his skin again. Ellie is his first love, and his last for a long time. When she turns to walk through the gate and fly back to Maryland and he exits the airport and heads to the boat that will take him farther south, their paths will diverge into separate universes. She will return to the Chesapeake, looking both inward and back through time, focusing through a microscope at organisms of the Tidewater region – and her personal and professional life will be nurtured by roots extending down through generations entrenched in those low sandy shores. He will spend the next few years journeying outward and all over the map, sailing seasonally with Uncle Norm in the tropics and getting a degree in linguistics up north. He'll study German and French and will be an exceptional student. He'll have an occasional short—term girlfriend. He'll fly to Europe. He'll go on to grad school and a good career. He'll spend summers with Norm aboard *Nightingale*, island hopping in the Caribbean and Central America. And he'll even traverse the Panama Canal one day and cross the Equator. Occasionally, he'll dream of Cape Horn.

When their eyes open, Stevie and Ellie know there's nothing else to say. This is when Ellie kisses him. This is where their story ends.

When a story ends with a long goodbye and a kiss in an airport, you can bet on it being over once and for all. There will be tears and nose—blowing and public emoting. There may be last—minute jitters: *don't go.* There will be onlookers looking on. But that's not where this story ends, because this is not the story you think it is. Sure, it's the story of a boy about to light out for new territory. It's the story of a boy and a girl who've both been lost, just a little, whose love has grown from grief and brought them here, to the domestic departures gate of the Miami International Airport. It's a story of friendship, too: Stevie, Ellie and Manny. An alliance deepened by remembrances of a friend gone forever and a common history reaching deep into the soil in which they buried him on a cold February day.

But this is not only a story about all that. This is also a story of a small girl who has spent the year not exactly in the middle of the story but somehow, strangely, at the heart of it — a girl growing up too, with dreams of her own.

Stevie is not choked up. He's saying goodbye to Ellie, but he's smiling. He's remembering every detail of her body, her hair, her eyes, her hands. And he's happy.

But when Sylvie pulls on his sleeve and gently tugs him down to her level, when he drops his backpack from his shoulder and kneels to look her in the eye, something breaks inside. She is not crying, but when she hugs him hard he feels his face wet with tears. His. Her lemony hair tickles his nose and the year washes over him. There's no sequence to it, but it's all there, from the car crash and Lucky's funeral to Ellie standing naked in his bedroom and Manny swan diving (also naked) off a dock on the South River. And there's this small girl, too — the girl who befriended him one rainy day when she asked him to help her bury her canary. The girl with no family other than a sister to get to school each morning. The girl who served him mac 'n' cheese on china plates and drank lemonade from Waterford crystal. The girl who gave him a bottle of sand from the beach and dirt from her own back yard to carry with him on his journey.

The girl who makes him cry.

"Hey, you know what?" he sniffs and pulls away, placing his hands on Sylvie's shoulders. "I met a boat with two kids on board — two small girls, one your size. Their boat is canary yellow."

"Really?"

"Yeah. And they eat cake off china plates."

"Well, it shouldn't be eaten any other way."

Stevie and Ellie laugh. Sylvie is an old soul, but she seems downright grandmotherly in her exactitude about cake etiquette.

"Yeah," Stevie stands as he continues. "We went and visited one day — Norm was borrowing some charts — and the mom served coffee in small white cups with silver trim, and plates with tiny grey flowers around the edges. She said it's her grandma's china, and she's had it with her all the time they've been sailing."

"Nice mom. I guess she knows how to keep things safe."

"Yeah," marvels Stevie. "Not a single one broken."

§

When the two sisters disappear down the corridor, when he can't see Ellie and Sylvie any longer, Stevie lets out a long sigh and turns on his heel.

Time to let them go. Time to go.

He's back on board *Nightingale* within an hour, tucked into his snug berth. He has not slept much in the past four days. Long days with Sylvie and Ellie, even longer nights with Ellie. He is worn out, body and heart. But he's also exhilarated. He can't fall asleep, so he pulls a book from his shelf: *Beautiful Swimmers*. A gift from Ellie, secured just above his bunk with a few other favorites: *Huck Finn* and *Walden*, Vonnegut and Bukowski, a stack of old Marvel comics and the collected works of Emily Dickinson. Beside the books there are also a few other items from home: a small stuffed Sulley from Monsters, Inc (a pet he's had his whole life, tossed in his duffle bag by his kid brother), a harmonica he's promised himself he'll learn to play, a Baltimore Orioles cap, a carton of Lucky Strikes − a parting gift from Manny ("'cause what else you gonna do on the high seas? May as well smoke, yeah?") − and a photo of his family in a small wooden frame: Mom, Dad, Rob, him.

He doesn't even get to the bottom of the page before he's drifting through a layer of golden dust and floating on a distant ocean. He's on the bow of a boat, swaying up and down with the motion of the gentle swell. The dust is everywhere. He sees each individual particle, and they are beautiful. The air is warm and golden. Through the glow, off his starboard bow, a shape forms. A ship. A ship on tumultuous seas. He looks harder as a grey haze replaces the golden light. The sky darkens now and a chill runs through his bones. Stevie is afraid of the heaving sea. He is afraid of the shape in the clouds. Then it comes into view, suddenly, and he recognizes Great Grandpa Gus. Gus has been prowling Stevie's dreams for over a year, luring him to sea from his whaling ship somewhere in the Southern Ocean. He appeared during the car crash back in January, the event that took Lucky's life and spared Stevie's and set the whole year in motion. And now, he's waving.

But there are two figures there. Standing beside Gus is someone else. Stevie squints to see better but just then his boat heels hard and he has to hold on for balance. He grabs a stay and turns to see Norm at the wheel of *Nightingale*, smiling and shouting happily over the howling wind, "Ready about?"

Stevie jumps to the cockpit to trim the sheets as the boat's bow comes through the wind. He concentrates on the task just a few seconds, releasing the starboard sheet and winding the winch to bring the jib to port.

Nightingale has tacked away and is steering a new course.

Stevie scrambles to the starboard side again just in time to see the other boat's stern. And there's Gus, still waving. Stevie can't make out the name on the transom but the other man comes into view quite clearly now, standing beside Gus. Stevie sees his jeans tattered at the knee, his flannel shirt with a yellow smiley−face tee peeking from underneath, a joint hanging from his lips. He's grinning and waving. A stupid, happy grin.

Lucky. Fuckin' Lucky. Dead Lucky.

Stevie hesitates, hears his heartbeat pierce the deafening wind. In one flash of a moment he feels guilty−angry−sad−pitiful−scared−relieved ... and something akin to happy. He can't help himself now − he grins back at his friend. And waves.

And then, the other ship is gone and the heaving seas settle. The black clouds disappear and *Nightingale* sails south by southwest over a glassy sea. The air is sparkling with that golden dust again. Stevie sees each tiny particle. In this one moment, in this dream, everything is beautiful.

Time to go. Time to let go.

§

On the northbound plane, Sylvie watches small ice crystals forming on the window. She sees each individual one, and they are beautiful. She leans her head into her sister's shoulder and falls to sleep. She sleeps hard most of the flight and it's only when Ellie nudges her awake that she remembers she's on a plane. In her dream, the vibrations and whirs of jet engines were blocked out. There was no turbulence, no crackling captain's voice with weather and geography updates. There was no one but her. She thinks she glimpsed Stevie once – but only for a moment and the moment's gone. In her lullaby dream, she was a particle of dust over a cornfield in a storm cloud, spinning dark and angry like something out of Kansas, then she was a drop of water in the sky, raining down into an endless golden ocean. Then – the way it happens in dreams – she was somehow herself again, a small girl gently rocking on a southbound boat, canary yellow, with china plates tucked safely in the cupboard.

Cracked
by Len Kuntz

Sunday, 14th December 2014

It's not even dawn. I'm broke, somewhere in the middle of East Jesus, Wyoming, and all the radio will pick up is twangy honkytonk or stations playing rambunctious Mexican music. Not only that, but my gas gauge is leaning its elbow on E.

This little joy ride of mine — almost a year now — has been an adventure, but it's done nothing to transport me out of the funk of having been dumped by my wife. If anything, I feel worse than when I first set out. Seeking adventure is fine, so long as you have a safe harbor to return to afterward. Without an anchor somewhere, a man might as well keep driving, fly his car right off a cliff, or drink himself dead.

The dashboard lights up in the far right corner, flashing strawberry red: *Get gas now!*

I'm not sure what to do. I check my wallet and pockets. I've got a buck twenty. That'd get me a third of a gallon of gas. But I need to eat because I'm starving.

Get gas now!

The landscape is a shroud of darkness. I'm going to run out of gas and die in the desert, be eaten alive by lizards. Panic sets in, as if termites have invaded my chest and are trying to gnaw their way through my flesh.

I try to keep my eyes off the dashboard but it's like trying to ignore your favorite pornography rippling across a computer screen.

Get gas now!

A spark of rage ambushes me. I feel the urge to break something, hurt someone, leave a life in ruins.

Get gas now!

Up ahead, the craggy, bone–dry land shows the semblance of a town coming into view – barn–shaped buildings and flat–topped domes.

I pull off at the first exit. It's December and chilly yet my armpits are drenched and I reek.

I find the gun in the cubby and tuck it between my waistband and belly. I have no idea what I'm doing but as soon as I enter the AM/PM mini mart the smell of scorched wieners reminds me that I'm ravenous.

I grab a basket and fill it with Ho Hos and Hostess fruit pies (cherry and chocolate) and toss in a six–pack of Budweiser and some Doritos and aspirins and bags and bags of beer nuts, plus rolls of SweeTARTS and an enormous sack of gummy bears.

At the counter, the teller rings the items up as if in a trance. He's got a shaved head, a stud through his nose, and gauges the size of quarters in his earlobes.

"Thirty–seven fifty–nine," he says, without looking me in the eye.

I whip out the pistol and point it at his forehead where a yoke–yellow pimple stares back at me.

"Hand me the money in the till."

"Are you shitting me?"

"I'm going to be shooting you in a second."

"There's a camera," he says, calm as can be, pointing up over his right shoulder.

"Do I look like I give a shit?" I jiggle the snout of the gun at him, hoping he doesn't notice that my hand is shaking.

"Suit yourself," the kid says, bored as death, stuffing bills into a brown paper bag that might have once contained his lunch.

"Change, too," I say, feeling greedy and desperate, thinking if I'm going to go through with this, I might as well get it all.

"Where's the duct tape?" I ask.

"Duct tape? We don't have no duct tape."

"Fine, then step around and get on your knees."

"There's no way I'm giving you a blow job."

"You're getting a little wishful," I say. "I need to tie you up."

When I cock the gun, it makes a teeth–scritching noise, and the kid obliges.

Once he's on the floor, I realize I don't have anything to tie him up with. I am probably the worst criminal ever.

"On second thought, get up. Give me the keys and your cell phone."

The guy hands them over. His phone cover is a Hello Kitty logo. "It's my sister's," he says, reading my expression. "I dropped mine in the toilet."

I lock him in the back office and stuff a stool up against the door knob so there's no way he's getting out on his own. I grab my money and goodies and fly out the door, waving at the camera on the way.

The only other car in the lot is the kid's and so I take it instead of mine. His is a vintage Volkswagen Rabbit, painted purple, that smells like a combination of Lysol and sweaty feet. Surprisingly, the gas tank is full. Surprisingly, the car has some guts.

I head west doing ninety–five, keeping my eyes peeled for lurking state troopers. My idea is to go as far as I can until the gas runs dry, then catch a bus. I figure it's the last place the cops would be looking for me, and besides, all they know is what the kid can tell them. My image on that camera won't do a bit of good.

I take a big bite of a cherry fruit pie, pop open a can of beer and take a swig to wash the fruity taste down. I'm feeling confident now, burning with a felonious high. It's the best I've felt all year. Even though I've committed a crime, I've accomplished something, something brave and daring. I wonder if my wife would be proud or scared or what. I wonder why I still care about her and what she thinks of me. Her new guy is probably doing her doggy–style right now.

Then I get a picture of her and him in bed, him mounted behind my wife, grunting and thrusting. My eyes sting. As I cross the border into Idaho, I start to bawl. It's only the second time I've cried in a decade, but now that I've started I can't stop. I don't know who I am or what I'm doing. I think about the gun I've stashed in the kid's glove compartment, next to his book of cigarette rolling papers. I could blow my brains out and not have to worry about my next move or how to make something of my life. I could fly off the curve up ahead where the road winds around a mountain. I've got a hundred different choices, and none of them are good.

It's nightfall and I'm on a Greyhound bus seated next to a young man with two prosthetic arms. I want to ask how he got them, how he lost his others. When he catches me staring, I shift in my seat and stare out the black window.

"IED," he says. "Afghanistan."

I look back. He's actually grinning.

"Could have been a lot worse," he says. "The guy that actually stepped on it, PFC Raymond Williams from Kentucky, he lost everything."

"God, I'm sorry."

"It's true what they say; war is hell."

"But you made it out."

"Most of me did. I'm thankful for that."

I feel a sense of shame wash in. Here I've been feeling sorry for myself all year and this guy lost two of his arms yet wears a bright smile.

We make small talk for the next hour. When I tell him I robbed a convenience store earlier today, he laughs. Nothing seems to faze him.

So I tell him about my last year, how I've been searching for something all this time since my wife left me.

"That's a shitty deal, a woman cheating on a guy. Not much worse, but you've got a choice to make."

"Yeah?"

"You can let it haunt you forever or else burn all your memories of her and start fresh."

"Is that what you did, with your experiences in the war?"

"I guess so. Of course, I've got these two reminders," he says, lifting his fake arms.

I feel guilty again for all my self-pity, yet it's easy to say, *burn all your memories*, and another thing doing it.

"Look," the guy says, "it's your life and who am I to say, but maybe what you went searching for was something that was in you all along."

"Like what?"

He punches me lightly in the chest with his fake fist. "Heart."

I'm not sure what he means exactly, but all the same he's got me thinking about courage and renewal.

The bus driver comes on the speaker telling us we're twenty minutes from Seattle.

"Say, did you really rob a convenience store?"

"Yeah," I say.

"Man, you're a real crack up."

Cracked, I think, but with luck and a lot of hard work, fixable.

Twelfth Inning
by Michael Webb

Monday, 15th December 2014

I drive the babysitter home, drink a diet cola in the kitchen, then sneak upstairs, trying not to wake the kids, padding into the bedroom in socks. Angela is facing away from me, looking at her reflection in a full–length mirror. She is topless, wearing only soft green sleep pants that ride low on her hips. I watch her turning, looking at her body in profile, and then straight, and then turning the opposite way. I stand and watch her. She seems focused on her belly, the gentle swell that rises below her ribs and above her wide hips. Despite our bickering now and then, she still makes my heart stop. Angela puts her hands behind her back then, pulling her shoulders back, her breasts full and round in front of her. Two children, but still as beautiful as a postcard, as precious as a love song.

"Hey," I say softly.

"Hey," she says. "Marcy proposition you yet?"

"Of course," I say, "you know I'm always beating her off with a stick." Our babysitter Marcelline, the 15–year–old daughter of one of the trainers at Athletes Performance Center, has become a running joke between us, after an offhand comment I made about how mature she looked. Angela now teasingly insists that she is about to seduce me every time we are alone for more than 30 seconds.

"As long as you keep that stick handy," she says. She turns to face me, her breasts sagging but full, glorious and round, her nipples enormous and brown. Angela's hands are still behind her back for another second, then she exhales, roundness returning to her stomach again. She walks across and into our bathroom.

"Did you talk to Jacob? He said he'd try you on your cell."

Jacob Feinberg, of Feinberg Sports Management LLC, is my agent. He is busy fielding and evaluating the offers for my services for next year, and hoping for the largest number possible that he can then take 10 percent of.

"I did," I say. I hear her brushing her teeth, so I continue. "He told me Seattle called, and Houston, and Cleveland made an offer. He's going to wait a few more days, and then if nobody blows him away, he thinks we should go with Seattle."

"Is it a good offer?" she asks with her mouth full of toothpaste.

"Pretty good. Three years. It will be nice to not be going hat in hand for a while. And the money is good, because I may not get another long one like this."

I hear her spit. "Sure you will," she says cheerfully.

"I appreciate your confidence," I say. "But the list of 35–year–old pitchers making big money is … well … it's not long, love."

"I'm sure you'll be on it," she says. I hear her washing her face. As I sit on the bed, with the bathroom door open a crack, I can still catch flashes of her bare skin as she moves around. I spy on her openly, still as thrilled as a 12–year–old who finds the hole in the fence where the neighbor's wife is sunbathing. Even with folds and wrinkles, perhaps because of them, she is still the most beautiful woman I have ever seen. I feel the throb under my pelvis. Maybe tonight, I think. We make love a fair amount, but I'm never averse to more.

She comes out, her face slightly red but looking clean and smooth, droplets adhering to stray hairs that circle her face like a halo. I feel need for her, acute and full, watching her hips sway as she walks across the bedroom. She slides her pants off her legs, leaving them beside the bed in case of some kid−fueled night time crisis.

"Are they good?" she says.

"Seattle?" I say. "No. They're young. Lots of promise. But they won't contend until the end of this contract, if even then. Lots of handholding, showing kids the ropes. Which sucks, but for the money they're offering, I'll do whatever they want."

"Oh," she says. She turns out the light on her side of the bed, then climbs under the covers. She finds her usual spot, her head resting on my chest, my hand down her back, her thigh thrown over mine. It is a subtle negotiation. Neither of us like to say no, even when that is the answer.

I spread my fingers out wide, feeling the muscles of her lower back and the delicate curve of her buttocks. Smelling her is an intoxicant. I think about the line I love from Joyce, about her name being a "summons to all my foolish blood," and the desire for her runs through me like a current. I can feel myself getting full, and growing, and beginning to press against the skin of her thigh.

"Oh," she says, swallowing a chuckle. "Hello there."

"Hi," I say. She shifts against me, opening her legs, her softness now on my skin, wet and intensely hot.

"I'd say someone wants something," she says. She moves her thigh slowly, rubbing the soft inside against the outside of me, a delightful torment.

"Someone wants something," I say, my voice growing thick. "That's for sure."

"Are you ready for another baby?" she asks me, her tone serious for a moment.

At this point, I felt hard pressed to refuse. I would say anything to get her to agree to what I want. I still don't think it is a good idea, but as my mother likes to remind me, not to decide is to decide.

"If you are," I say. She slides herself on top of me, getting into position, lifting one leg slightly to guide me into place. I ache for her now, feeling lust and greed filling my head like popcorn in a bag.

"Good," she says, letting me have her, her weight coming down as I slide inside her, strong and velvety smooth and wet, surrounding me delightfully in our practiced rhythm. I sigh with pleasure.

She groans. "Good," she says again, "I tested this morning. I'm pregnant."

Alive and Kicking
by James Claffey

Tuesday, 16th December 2014

The Shannon burst its banks a week ago and sheep, cattle and the odd goat float bloated and lost in the middle of Ireland's great start−up lake. Farmers wring their hands in McKettrick's snug, drowning their sorrows and totting up the EU compensation they'll collect in the New Year. The Bird knows plenty of them will invent numbers the way the government seems to do on an almost daily basis in order to put a rosy look on the unemployment figures. Only the prior Monday he started a new course in Athlone at the technical college, a Postgraduate Diploma in Business in Cultural Event Management. He likes the sound of it and daydreams about leading large groups of foreign travelers about the countryside searching for fairy forts and Leprechaun troves. He also conjures up the idea of a lovely single French woman to replace Melodie in his heart's desire.

This afternoon the nuns are all in a dither about the visit of the Archbishop to the convent. Bunting and flags are put into place and the narrow triangular fabric that last saw air when the Pope visited in the 1980s now adorns the railings of the church grounds. A great honor, the Mother Superior told the Bird when he inquired as to the occasion. If he can have the Archbishop's ear for a minute, the Bird will put a stop to the Mother

Superior's gallop and tell the man about the nun's swindling ways and property acquisitions. Shite and onions, the Bird thinks, as the bloody Church is as crooked as the road to Baltrasna. He left the nuns in "high Do" and wished the miseries of the world to be heaped on their crow-like shoulders.

Maybe he'll whitewash the doors of the convent with the words, 'Thieving Bitches', or worse?

In the dim light of the snug he orders another Guinness and watches the dark liquid settle in the glass, layers of time collapsing on top of one another. No one speaks to him and he sups alone and unhappy in the corner. The racing from Kempton Park is on the television and a horse takes a terrible fall as the Bird watches the final furlong unfold. Maybe that's how his own life will end, in a tragic fall, legs broken, heart pounding out the last desperate beats. Worse ways to die, he thinks, draining the Guinness and making for the door.

On the street a few hardy souls wait for the bus to Athlone, the wind blowing hard and the spits of rain a promise of more to come. Those nuns, he ponders. "Don't tread on me," he whispers. Yes, he'll show those crones who the boss is when push comes to shove. Hands thrust in his pockets as he walks, the Bird pushes into the wind and makes towards the river to see what might be floating by in the water.

A trip to Clara to listen to the music isn't out of the question, and the Bird lingers on the picture in his head of the lovely French girl he might have wooed had fate not slapped him for his insolence. Melodie. She was some looker and no mistake, he thinks. The time she almost smothered him between her breasts, and him as useless as a broom on a beach to clean up the sand.

As he steps out the door of the house to cycle over to Clara, the Bird stops to gaze up past the rooftops of the town. The velvet December sky gives the Bird some solace, though, so many pinpricks of light shining in the heavens. Love is not something he's had much luck with, one way or the other, and he wishes it were different, but at least he'd had a sliver of opportunity with Melodie, until he'd scared her away with his talk of the Mammy's ghost.

The river is fast flowing, bushes and branches of downed trees tumble by as the Bird flies by with the breeze on his back. Fast out, slow home, he thinks. Across the wide expanse of water lights flicker in the night. Maybe cottages of farmers cut off by the high floodwater. Or, maybe, faeries afoot on these last nights of the last month of the year? He'll have to keep a wide berth of any of the supernatural creatures abroad, and with his own mammy prone to dropping by unannounced, the Bird is no stranger to the weirdness of this life.

Hogan's is packed to the rafters and the Bird doesn't recognize any of the musicians tonight. Melodie might be back in France for the holidays, or off with her damned boyfriend, the fortunate cur.

As he takes a seat by the bar a hand on his shoulder startles him and he prays it's Melodie, but Father O'Hehir's sober face stares at him. "Bird, isn't it well you're looking?"

"How are you, Father?"

"Never better. Though I'll be mightily relieved when the Archbishop is come and gone. That Mother Superior has me driven distracted by her constant phone calls about this, that, and the other."

"Can I buy you a drink, Father, for the holidays?" The Bird lifts a hand to hail the barman.

"A small whiskey, thanks very much." The priest sidles into the spot next to the Bird and plants his behind on the stool. "I prefer the company of men, Bird," he says. "Not that there's anything wrong with the fairer sex, but sometimes I don't have the patience for all their insignificant blather."

The Bird shrugs, lifting the glass to his lips. "*Sláinte*, and a *Nollaig Shone Dhuit*," he says to the priest.

"And to yourself, Bird. May the coming year bring you better luck than this one did."

The reels and jigs commence and the two men turn their backs to the bar, feet tapping along with the music. Voices join in the chorus of the songs that play between the dancing tunes and for a moment the Bird imagines his life not to be too shabby after all. Across the room the musicians sit in a semi−circle, instruments blazing, cigarette boxes on the table ready for their break. A middle−aged woman pours sweat and wrists the *bodhrán*, her eyes tightly shut, the strains of a familiar tune filling the air. The Bird recalls the music Melodie played the first night he saw her in here, and he draws a deep breath and believes he can catch her scent still lingering in the pub.

Nothing in his life is the way he wants it, not work, not love, not family, and least of all not Melodie. The Bird shifts on his stool, only realizing the priest is no longer beside him, and he searches the room for the man. Never around when you need one, he thinks. He raises his hand to order again and when he turns back to face the music he feels the beginnings of a tear traveling down his cheek.

"Would you send over a drink to the woman playing the *bodhrán*, like a good fellow," the Bird tells the barman. When the set ends the barman delivers the Bird's gift and says something to her. The woman raises her eyebrows and lifts the glass to the Bird in thanks. "Sláinte," she mouths, silently, winking at him. In return the Bird raises his own drink to her and says, "Alive and kicking. Alive and kicking." He slips off the stool and makes his way across the packed bar to the players, a battered old boat navigating the choppy and dangerous waters of life and love. The Bird shouts, "My name is Mahony, the Bird Mahony, nice to meet you."

"By the hokey, that's a name worth remembering," she tells him. "Rose. Rose Conroy."

The Bird feels the leaky boards of his craft lighten a bit. He pulls at his ear, grins, and realizes he has some living to take care of before he too fades and sinks beneath the overflowing Shannon waters.

What It Feels Like
To Have Your Friends
Dying Around You
by Gwendolyn Joyce Mintz

Wednesday, 17th December 2014

Mora makes her way across the parking lot to the front door of Kelly's, all the while telling herself to go elsewhere. At the threshold, she stops and gives the idea serious consideration.

"But I promised Aaron," she says aloud, her words a whispered white breath in the cold air.

She pulls the door open.

Another time, her heart would have been tugged by the deep green wreaths and garland decorating the walls and doors. The mistletoe placed strategically above the hostess podium might have made her smile. The boisterous rendition of 'Joy to The World', one of her favorite songs, blaring through the speakers might have had her joining in. *And Heaven and Nature Sing.* Another time –

She heads straight for the bar where she orders a glass of champagne. The bartender takes her money and is about to leave but Mora stops him by holding out one hand. Tossing her head back, she downs the drink. She pushes the empty champagne flute across the bar counter.

"Another one," she tells the bartender. "And some water."

She pays for the second glass, and then takes her drinks to a nearby cocktail table to sit.

She watches the servers interacting with patrons and she wonders if Lindsey is working. She hopes she is and she hopes she isn't.

Lindsey wasn't working when the group last met.

It was then Aaron had announced, "This is gonna be my last meeting."

"You're finally doing it?" Phil had asked.

"Yep."

Aaron was heading out of town for the Thanksgiving holiday, to Dallas, where his parents lived.

"Decide how?" Phil had continued.

Aaron had had a paper napkin in his hands and he had folded it and then again. Again. Unfolding it, he had said, "Did you know you can search the internet for quick ways to die? I always meant to tell you guys about this one site ..."

His attention had drifted to the tables around them. Then he'd slowly turned back to them. He'd tossed the napkin toward the center of the table and said, "Guns are messy. Pills take too long. Some other ways invite your body to fight for survival, and from what I've read, the struggle is not pretty. So it's down to carbon monoxide –"

"Your car is being picked up by the new owner after the meeting," Mora had interjected.

Aaron had frowned. "It wouldn't've worked anyway, low emission. But my father has two cars. Old ones. And a garage." Aaron had picked the napkin up again and began twisting it tight. "And then there's hanging."

"Seriously? You weren't disturbed by that book in high school – the way they described John hanging there? Why would anyone wanna leave that kind of image in someone else's mind?"

78

Aaron's sigh had been loud enough to have people from other tables turn to them. "Mora —"

"I'm sorry," she'd quickly said.

"You don't have to be here."

She'd said she did. "I promised to be with you guys to the end."

"Then you're going to need to shut up," Phil had told her.

Later, when Aaron sent the text, he used a previous thread that had been a group message. When Phil sent a response to Aaron, telling him that he had been a good friend and that perhaps it was time for him to check out as well, Mora got a copy.

She got a copy of Aaron's reply to Phil and then Phil's next reply. There were a few more texts and then Aaron sent one that said, "Unfortunately, this was not a *fan* club. Goodbye."

Phil sent another. "Later."

And then the texting stopped.

It was only days ago that Mora was able to take a deep breath and search for their obituaries online. She left a comment in both of the visitor books although she believed what she'd written was trite in the face of what she knew.

"Hey?"

Mora blinks and she's out of her thoughts and back in the restaurant.

Lindsey is standing there.

"Hey, hi," Mora says.

"You alone?"

Mora nods. "No one else could make it."

"Can I get you something? This isn't my section and I'm off in a few minutes but I could run an order in for you."

"I'm fine," Mora says, "but thanks."

"Just here to celebrate?"

"Huh?"

Lindsey points at the champagne flute. "Someone in your club has accomplished their goal."

Mora tilts the flute slightly and twirls the remaining champagne around. "Yeah, something like that."

Tell her.

Mora sets the glass upright and looks at Lindsey. "Can I talk to you before you leave?"

"Sure. I'll be right back."

Mora nods.

When Lindsey returns, she drapes her coat over the back of a chair and sits down. She slips the elf cap off her head and shoves it into her purse which she sets on the table.

"I hope you get paid extra for that," Mora tells her.

Lindsey grins. "We do, but it's fun too." Her hands smooth the sides of her green costume. "Unfortunately it's impossible to find non–slip, pointy–toed shoes so the look is just a bit off." She lifts her foot and wiggles it. "But you wanted to talk to me."

"I was wondering if Aaron ever told you what our club was about."

"He said you met to talk about life and death matters."

Mora smiles and shakes her head. Aaron. "That's close. We were interested in suicide; we met to figure out how to die."

Lindsey's expression moves to stoic as her gaze sharpens on Mora. She nods as she begins to understand. "So, when someone didn't show up, it was because they were dead?"

"Yes."

Lindsey's eyes shoot to the champagne flute. When she speaks, it's slow like she's using words for the first time. "Is ... he ... dead?"

Should have used a buffer –

Mora is surprised by Lindsey's sudden tears. Maybe there had been more than Aaron said. "I'm sorry. I –"

"No, no," Lindsey tells her. "It's not like that." She swipes at her cheeks. "I liked you guys, you weren't just a tab." She takes a breath. A few more. "I'm from a small town and when I was in middle school, our town made the national news because our suicide rate was bigger than the nation's average. Kids were just killing themselves. My sister's friend. The boy next door. Our dad's boss's daughter." She takes the napkin Mora holds out to her and blows her nose. "Our parents got scared and they were always talking to us about it, to make sure we weren't considering it but they never asked what it felt like to have your friends dying all around you." She pulls strands of hair from her wet cheeks. "I just never dealt with it." Lindsey takes a breath. "Aaron is dead?"

Mora can't stop the tears that come to her eyes. "Yes. Phil too."

"Wow," Lindsey whispers. Wow, her mouth forms the word again. She leans back in the chair and stares at Mora. "Are you next?"

Mora shakes her head. She may not have the life she wants but she can live with the life she has. "I tried two times before to kill myself and while there are days I don't want to live, there are not days when I want to die."

"I'm sorry," Lindsey says, sliding off the chair and reaching for her jacket. "Thank you for telling me but I just can't do this right now."

From her seat, Mora places her hand on Lindsey's arm as Lindsey reaches for her purse sitting on the table. "This is hard, I know. But listen, since you're off, why don't we go somewhere else and talk?"

Flow
by Stephen V. Ramey

Thursday, 18th December 2014

The room is like a cathedral, dark panels, painted ceilings, brass everywhere. A polished bar runs the back half of one wall, bottles stacked along the mirror behind it. The tap is a glory of levers and logos.

You might wonder how Lanigan's Irish Pub ended up in a place like New Castle, with its Italian tradition and economic woes. While you're at it, you might wonder how a 50–something guy who never drank much, never smoked, was reasonably athletic, ended up with aggressive prostate cancer. You might wonder any number of things, but sometimes stuff just *is*.

"What do you say to another Guinness?" Jimmy says. He and Rose and Anne and I are sitting at a table, winter coats draped over our chairs.

"I say if you're not with us, you're a Guinness," I answer. It feels good to smile.

Jimmy rolls his eyes. "Leave the comedy to professionals."

"I think two is plenty," Anne says. "You have your appointment in the morning."

"They won't care if I'm hung over. It's the other end that concerns them." I signal to the server, avoiding Anne's glare. "Another round, please."

"What's this thing called again?" Jimmy says.

"Cyberknife," I say. "It's an experimental radiation protocol. I have to fill out the paperwork tomorrow."

"Cyberknife," Jimmy says. "That's cutting edge, right?" He stares at Rose as if expecting her to laugh.

Rose turns to me. "I'm sorry, Stephen. Sometimes I wish he came with an *OFF* button."

The server approaches in her plaid skirt that shows off those firm white thighs. *If only I was younger, and not dying.* She sets the drinks onto the table, one by one, and picks up the empties. Mine is in a wooden tankard.

Anne watches intently as if she's afraid I'll fall off my chair, or maybe forget my promise to fight this thing. It irks me that she would doubt me after what we went through with the cat, but it's a passing irk. A buzz has settled nicely into my brain. I drink once and set the tankard down.

"Let's go. I've had enough."

Outside, the air is sobering. The moon, a mere sliver, hangs above the parking lot. I pause to gather my bearings and a thought beams bright across my brain.

"When this all began," I say, "I went to the tent city along the river and spoke to a woman named Tomorrow. She told me to come back when I was —" I make air quotes "— *ready.*"

"Oh, how interesting," Rose says. "Why don't we take a stroll down there now?"

"It's darker than Obama's nutsack down there," Jimmy says.

"Afraid you'll fall in?" Rose says. She gets that playful look, wide doe eyes, brows arched.

Jimmy laughs. "I'm afraid you'll fall in and melt, you're so sweet."

"You're my Cinnabon." Rose pinches Jimmy's butt, then he's chasing her through the parking lot, across the street down the slanted path to the river.

Anne watches stoically, but I see a hint of smirk.

"Pathetic, isn't it?" I say.

"Let's pretend we don't know them," she says.

"Agreed." Holding hands, we stroll after our crazy friends. "Jimmy's a little drunk to be driving anyway."

We follow a path, graveled but not yet asphalted. Rose's laughter echoes beneath the bridge. When we reach the river bend, we find two coats hanging from a tree limb and two sets of shoes standing along the shore. Jimmy and Rose are splashing in the shallows.

"Aren't you guys freezing?" Anne says.

"No, it's fine," Jimmy says. "My wife's so hot the water's starting to boil."

"Come in," Rose says. "The waning is a perfect time for letting go."

"Of what?" I say.

"Of everything unnecessary." Rose slides her blouse over her head. Jimmy unbuttons his shirt.

"I'm not taking off my clothes," Anne says. "It's supposed to go down to thirty tonight."

I nod absently, but the truth is I do feel the river calling. *Come to me, Stephen, come…*

I sit on the bank and pull off a shoe. A Velcro rip staccatos. I remove the other more slowly, then my socks, roll up my pant legs until they're cuffed at my knees.

"You're not actually going in," Anne says.

"Why not?"

She watches Rose in her black brassiere, Jimmy bare-chested. Breath steams from their mouths.

"You're going to have to be careful once you start chemo," Anne says.

I stand. "I haven't started yet. Are you sure you won't come with me?"

She shakes her head stoically.

I leave my coat on in deference to her concern and step in. Icy water hits like a sledge. I gasp. Cold becomes numb, becomes a strange kind of warmth moving slowly up my legs, my hips, my spine, revealing me to myself. Healthy tissue glows. Disease is banded gray or black, a topography of linked valleys and mountain nodules. I shudder – there's so much – and then I think of Mystery breathing in and out with such resolve. *You can kill me, but I will not make it easy.*

The river flows around me, dark and steady. My hands dip reflexively into my pockets. I feel a keychain and pull it out. Dangling amid the keys is the flash stick Frank bought for me. My novel is stored on that drive, at least the portion written since Frank, which is most of it, really.

I turn, pulling the flash stick out from the keys to show Anne. "Remind me when we get home to save this –"

Something shoves me. My foot slips. Hands flailing, I fall. The flash stick twists. The key ring flies off. I hit the water with a cushioned splat. Tendrils of cold water flow across my hands and neck.

"Are you all right?" Rose and Jimmy splash over.

Jimmy's forearms hook my armpits and lift me up. Water dribbles from the hem of my coat.

"Can't take you anywhere," he says. He releases me, holding just long enough to make sure that I stand on my own in the water.

"Someone pushed me," I say. "Was it you?"

Jimmy extends his arms. "Do I look like Wilt Chamberlain?" His teeth chatter, and he starts toward the tree where their coats are hanging. "I'll get yours, Baby," he says over his shoulder.

"Thanks," Rose answers. Even in scant light I see the gooseflesh standing from her arms.

"I'm serious," I say. "I didn't fall, I was –"

"Let it go," Rose says. Her eyes tighten. "All of it, Stephen. The river wants you clean."

"Yeah, right. I suppose there's an app for that." The cold hits me, a shiver in my stomach that races to my shoulders. I turn. Anne has stepped into the stream, one shoe drenched, one pant leg wicking cold water. She's waiting for me to choose between Rose in the current and her by the shore.

"I'm coming," I say.

Rose grabs my arm and pulls me around as Jimmy drapes a coat across her shoulders and continues downstream. She cups my cheek. "You know I'm right."

A part of me does know, the part that danced with Amanda's ghost, the part that drew me to church that day and urged my disastrous walkabout. The part that slept while Mystery died on my stomach. My hand goes to the wound in my side, no more than a frowning white line after Frank's care.

I want so badly to wash away the diseases I've been running from, but it's a lie to think I can. There is no easy way out, no magic kingdom. *Breathe,* I think. *You can kill me, but I will not make it easy.* I think of a kitten on the palm of my hand, and a sob pushes up from my chest.

Rose nods at the moon. "The final phase," she says. "The letting go before rebirth." And then she's guiding me toward Anne, one arm draped across my shoulder. *Splat—splat—splat* our footsteps sound. My pant legs drag in the water.

Jimmy slaps up behind us. "Your keys." He presses a mass of rough edges into my hand. A half—moon plastic eyelet clings to the ring.

"The flash stick, where's the flash stick?"

Jimmy frowns. "Didn't see one."

I lunge for the river. Jimmy grabs my arm.

"You don't understand," I pant. "My book's on that drive."

Jimmy glances back. The river is darker than the sky. "We'll find it in the morning, okay? When there's more light. Don't you have it on your laptop?"

"No."

Jimmy squeezes my shoulder. "I have two things to say to you, Stephen. Backup." He squeezes again. "And backup."

"Jimmy ..." Rose warns.

"So, he'll write it again. I have to redo bits of my act all the time on the road. Usually they come out better."

"Fuck you, Jimmy." I shove, but he barely budges. "This isn't a joke, okay? It's my life on that disk, twelve chapters. Do you have any idea how long it took?"

"Let it go," Rose says. "Fight the battle you need to fight now."

I sigh. "All I ever wanted was to write one masterwork, something meaningful to leave behind."

"The perfect joke," Jimmy says. "I get that."

"No you don't," I say, and my stomach clenches. "No one 'gets it' Jimmy. You have Rose, you have your work, you fit in. I don't have any of that. I —"

"You have Anne," Rose says, and shame slams down like a block of ice. I look to my wife, standing forlornly by the bank.

"I didn't mean ... that didn't come out right." I remember her coming to me on the stairs when Mystery died. Have I thrown that away? What's wrong with me?

Anne's shoulders slump. She reaches out, flesh so white it all but glows. "Come," she says. I take her hand. She leads me from the river. "Believe it or not," she says while efficiently stripping the coat off my back. "I do understand you, Stephen."

Without the coat I feel even colder. I pull my arms tight as the shivering resumes. Anne opens her coat wide. For a moment, I'm confused, then I understand. I step closer, and she enfolds me. I think of our honeymoon beneath the stars, sharing a sleeping bag, her naked breasts pressed to me, want surging through my body in electric waves. I believed we would go into that bundle as separate people and emerge as one.

"Thank you," I whisper. I work my arms around Anne under her coat. She leans her forehead to mine. Life didn't work out the way we planned in retrospect, but who's to say it won't this time?

"This is what you should write about," Rose says. "You've had quite a year."

Indeed.

Families

by Gay Degani

Friday, 19th December 2014

On the creek side of the Old Road, the sun dips behind the wild growth of the arroyo and hills beyond, cooling the warm California afternoon. Jamie, sitting across from Gus German on the porch of his bungalow, stops shuffling cards, places them on the small table, and zips up her sweatshirt. She glances over at Lily and Collin, her two little kids rolling down the knoll of dirt and weeds where their bungalow used to stand before a giant oak, uprooted by 100 mile an hour winds, smashed it to matchsticks back in January.

"You gonna deal those things?" asks Gus, his dog Gracie propped on his lap. His voice is gruff, but Jamie knows he's harmless. Like so many old men who haven't lived with a woman for years, he's forgotten his softer, kinder voice. Of course, Gus may never have had that voice. He certainly doesn't have it for his son, Mars.

"Hey ho!" Sybil hollers as she emerges from her own bungalow.

Jamie twists in her seat. Laughs. "What've you got there?"

Gus mumbles under his breath and Gracie perks her head.

"Martinis! It should be egg nog, I know, but it's still too warm to break out the heavy stuff." Sybil moves carefully down her front stairs and starts across the courtyard. She's wearing one

89

of her sarongs, its slit up the side not quite high enough to allow for anything but geisha—girl steps. Jamie scoots out her chair and hurries to help, taking the loaded tray from Sybil when she reaches her.

Arriving at Gus's bungalow, Sybil asks, "How's Mars these days?"

The old codger doesn't answer, again making Jamie wonder why he hates to be around — let alone talk about — his son. Jamie says, "He's helping Ian flip a house over on the Northside."

When Sybil's eyebrows shoot up, Jamie knows what she's asking, with whose money, and shrugs. Sybil angles her chin toward Gus, but Jamie shakes her head as she puts the tray on top of the cards.

"Hey!" grouses Gus.

"Oh, have a drink," says Sybil.

Jamie does the duty, pouring martinis from the pitcher into small juice glasses. A jar of green olives perches on the edge of the tray, but no toothpicks, so she fingers out two, drops them in, and hands the first glass to Gus, which he takes, sniffs, then sips, a "Hmmmm" of reluctant satisfaction slipping out.

"He and Ian are doing it. Maybe Ian's mom lent them the money." Jamie pours one for Sybil and offers her the chair.

"Thank you, sweetie." The older woman sits and raises her glass to Gus. He grunts, raising his own in return, frowning at the tray still covering the cards.

Jamie plops onto the porch's top step, grins at her kids who are chasing around the weedy dirt where her own bungalow used to be. "What're you going to do with that spot, Sybil?"

"Not going to rebuild, that's for sure."

"We should plant a tree there," says Jamie. "A Christmas tree, and that way we can decorate it every year, right out there on the lawn."

"Christmas trees don't look good in people's yards," mutters Gus.

"What do you have against Christmas trees?" asks Sybil.

"I don't, but it'll stick out like a sore thumb all year long. Get one of those deodars they got up there north of town. Plant something like that."

"Those are too big. Maybe just a pine. A regular pine, the kind with long thick needles. We can still string lights on it." Sybil squints as she talks, like she's trying to visualize, then says to Jamie, "There're two juice boxes on the tray for the kids."

"I saw those. Thanks," says Jamie. "Don't want to call them over just yet. They're having so much fun. So strange to be back, Sybil. Thank you for letting us move into Mrs. Renke's."

"Not a problem. Glad you got back when you did."

"Oh good God," grunts Gus.

Jamie glances at the old man, his mouth a scowl.

Collin yells, "Mom, Mars is here!"

Of course. Gus's son. She doesn't understand it. Not really. Why Gus and Mars don't get along. When she'd first met Mars, he'd made her nervous with his beseeching eyes, and Gus seemed almost proud of him. Now almost a year later, he regards the man with what amounts to disgust.

Mars lifts Collin and swings him around, then follows the boy over to the mound of weedy dirt where they both get down on hands and knees. Lily scrunches her face, arms folded tight against her chest. Bugs, thinks Jamie. Collin and his bugs.

She glances at Gus. He's staring into his juice glass of vodka. What happened between the two while she and her kids had been away? A murder, for one, a neighbor woman strangled and dumped in the arroyo across the street. The cops picked up Mars because he was an ex−con, in prison for robbery, maybe more than one, but when they couldn't find any evidence he'd had anything to do with the murder, they let him go. Maybe Gus still believes he's the one, but Jamie doesn't think that's possible. Mars is kind and patient with the kids. He likes her and she's beginning to like him, but she's careful now. One failed marriage is enough.

When Mars stands, he brushes dirt from his pants and waves. Jamie waves back. The kids race toward the porch. Gus bolts up, his face purpling, knocking over the table, tray and glasses crashing to the porch floor. With Gracie in his arms, he stumbles into his bungalow and slams the door.

Handing the kids their juice boxes, Jamie sends them back to their bugs. As soon as they're gone, she helps Sybil clean up the mess, crouching down, tossing shards of glass onto the tray, not wanting to look at Mars. He says, "I should go."

"No you shouldn't," says Sybil. She touches Jamie's head and turns to pound on Gus's front door, saying, "I'm coming in, you old coot."

Once Sybil's inside, the door closed, Jamie looks at Mars, whispers, "Has he always been this way?"

"Let's talk on your porch."

Sitting on the bottom steps, Jamie and Mars watch the kids march around the courtyard in a game of follow–the–leader, Collin matching each of his sister's hops, jumps, and arm waves.

Without looking at Mars, Jamie asks, "So why is your father so –"

"Angry with me?"

Her eyes meet his, and she realizes she wants there to be a compelling explanation.

"He blames me for my mother's death."

"Why?"

The streetlights glow up and down the Old Road as a breeze rustles through the neighbor's camphor tree. Jamie hugs her knees.

Finally he says, "I don't know. I liked to take things. Steal things. I was always in trouble. Don't really know why. Ran away from home a couple times. Didn't finish anything I started. Maybe I was ADD. I don't know."

Jamie shivers, waits. The kids lie still on the lawn, talking, giggling.

"So I was fifteen, I got this girl pregnant. You have to understand. My mother, she went to Mass every day, ran the women's league, sewed altar cloths, and she was humiliated. She locked herself in the bedroom and wouldn't come out. I ran away. I don't know which shamed her more, having a bastard in the family or a coward for a son. She took a bunch of pills. They couldn't save her. Gus. He found me, beat me up, dragged me to the funeral."

Jamie rests her hand on his arm. Squeezes. Still he doesn't look at her.

"When I was eighteen, I left and we didn't talk to each other for years. Then when he got sick, I came back and we got along for a while, but I wasn't ready to change yet. That's when I ended up in jail. That stint cured me. I think it cured me."

They sit in silence a moment or two, then the kids run up, blond hair haloed by moonlight. Jamie reaches out and gathers them close, Collin wrestling with her a little bit, but giving in. She turns to Mars. Their eyes meet again and she says, "Well, I guess we'll see, won't we?"

A stranger jogs along the Old Road, his attention drawn by the sound of voices. He slows, then stops, leaning over to rest hands on knees, breathing in and out, turning his head to stare at the family on the porch of one of four bungalows. They bunch close together as the woman points to the starry sky, the moon shining across her face. Jamie.

He smiles at the sudden hardness inside his running shorts and as he stands there, he slips his right hand inside. He won't make himself wait this time. He's waited long enough.

Feliz Navidad
by Sally—Anne Macomber

Saturday, 20th December 2014

T **o:** Milton Flaxmill, Red Cow Publishing
From: Trudy Polaris
Date: December 20, 2014 10.19 p.m.
Re: Peek—a—boo

Øslø was a bust! How was I to know they give the *Peace Prize*
in Øslø, and all the *other* Nobel Prizes in Støckhølm!? So I
missed out, completely. Maybe next year will be better for me. I
heard on the street and also in the corridors of the King Kristian
XVII Hotel and then again on the ferry across the Øslø Fjørd to
Høvedøya that they never give it to you for your first
nomination anyway. Thank God I did not waste my Red Cow
Publishing future expense account on that tacky ocelot dress.

And no, I didn't even check to see who won the awards I was
up for, Literature and Physics, but they were probably won by
someone unimportant and stupid and I am not bothered that I
do not know who they might be. It matters not one whit. The
future holds much brighter circumstances for me.

Some other news: my husband is in the local psychiatric hospital
for tax evasion, back in the Tyrol. He's getting the best care the
low Austrian schilling can give him.

I am also wondering if maybe the Himalayas (ie *Nuclear Fission in The Himalayas*) are a little ambitious for my *first* book. Maybe the sheer magnitude of those mountains turned the Nobel judges against me, you know, the new kid in town getting too big for her boots already. So a rethink on the Himalayas versus Pyrénées issue would be a good thing. *Definitely* a good thing. Something smaller and subtler would be advisable. Maybe the Pyrénées are too big too.

What do you know about the Dolomites?

I have to say Boston is so *lovely* in the lead–up to Christmas!

As the year draws to a close, I find myself reflecting on the last 12 months and I can't help but marvel at the resilience of the human spirit in the face of countless setbacks. Or continued neglect. More specifically, *my* resilience in the face of countless setbacks and continued neglect. 12 months of being ignored? In my book, that's a record!

The greatest Christmas gift you could give me would be a sign from you – maybe even a meeting.

There was no plaque on the building when I arrived at 10.00 this morning here on Mount Vernon Street, but a sixth sense told me that Red Cow Publishing is on the 6th floor. I walked in and was surprised to see the receptionist wearing white, disguised as a dental nurse.

She said Red Cow Publishing had gone bankrupt and left Boston, maybe even left the planet but I know that behind that sterile white door there's a lot of book publishing activity going on. Even on a Saturday. *Especially* on a Saturday. I could smell the printer's ink disguised as amalgam!

I told nursey I wanted an appointment to get my teeth cleaned, and sat down while she pretended to look on the computer and book me an appointment. So I just hung around for a while in the waiting room and when I knew she wasn't looking (because her white cap had disappeared behind the computer screen — I am sure she was feeding her smack habit when she thought I couldn't see her!) I snuck into the restroom (as you so quaintly call them here), hid in the storage cupboard and that's where I am now, 12 hours later.

Luckily I brought my mega—foldable camp stove with me and a blow up—sleeping bag and astronaut food pills (along with my laptop, of course!) and once I sign off this email I'll get the kinks out of my back and set up camp on the restroom floor.

I'll be here when you get in first thing Monday morning.

We may even have shaken hands by the time you open this email!

I'm easy to spot. I'll be the one waiting for you in the waiting room. With the laptop on my lap. And just in case a lot of your "patients" have laptops on their laps, I'll be the one sitting under the mistletoe with the Christmas sombrero on my head.

See you very very soon, Milton, and — oh, how I can't wait! — in full sound and 3D!

Much love,

Trudelein xx

PS: It would be best to cancel all your appointments for Monday morning, as we really do need to knock the editing of my book, whatever it's going to be called, on the head.

Cruisin' on a Sunday Afternoon
by Mandy Nicol

Sunday, 21st December 2014

My heart's racing, I'm short of breath.

I watch the clouds through the window and wish I could gulp in some fresh air. I imagine I'm walking in the bush with Peregrine who's racing around barking at startled rabbits and cockatoos and blue tongue lizards. It doesn't help.

The guy on my right keeps fidgeting and sighing and checking his watch. He's not helping either.

I didn't think I'd be like this.

I had no fear of flying.

So maybe I'm worried about something else. What if I don't like Sydney? What if I don't like bobbing around on the ocean? What if I don't like the job? What if I don't *have* a job? What if I misunderstood? What if I've made it all up? What if I am mad?

I snatch my new iPhone out of my bag, fiddle around to find the text:

> *Nadia when can U get here? Get passport sorted.*
> *Want to pop U on Noumea cruise Jan. nevil wu*

I *do* have a job. I make a snorty chuckling noise and the guy on my right peers at me with his nose screwed up like I'm another of his problems. If he didn't look like an angry camel I'd tell him all about my job. How I stumbled across it on the internet:

> *Expert tailor / dressmaker wanted for fitting and*
> *making alterations to show costumes for cast*
> *members on board cruise ships.*

It sounded like a career you dream about. Apparently cruise ships stage a great variety of shows these days, from Broadway plays and musicals to Aqua Theatre. I could be paid to help people dress up like pirates and princesses while cruising around the ocean visiting tropical islands.

So I sent off my portfolio to Nevil Wu Costume Designs.

And then I realised I'd have to move to Sydney.

But I convinced myself that I wouldn't get the job so I didn't need to worry about it.

And then Nevil Wu rang and raved about my work and his work and how much fun it all was working with fabric and colour and actors and theatre and how he could use me as a designer as well and we may in fact turn out to be kindred spirits and did I believe in kindred spirits and when I said yes he said see there you go I knew it and when I said I didn't know a soul in Sydney so how could I possibly move there he said pffft and gave me contacts for share houses in Lilyfield and Camperdown so I said yes I'll come as soon as I can.

When I told Mum she surprised me. She smiled and gave me a hug.

We had an early Christmas and Farewell Nadia family do.

Celeste said I was mad, leaving everything I know for God Knows What and So Far Away. Then she asked what discount I get for family.

Anthony said I'm a crazy lunatic acting like a ten–year old kid running off to join the circus. Which I sort of *am*. I think he was mostly bummed because he had me pegged as housekeeper for his newly envisioned Agri–Tourism arm of his Grand Farm Revamp.

Mum told him to stop ragging me. Told him I was obviously a creative genius – ok, she might not have said genius – and that he should be happy for me. Told him it was high time I got out and saw the world. Told him if you stay in the same spot too long you get pins and needles. Then she told him to put the kettle on.

It was at that moment that I thought I might miss her, one day.

I know I'll miss Peregrine but at least he's attached himself to Anthony so I hope he won't miss me too much.

I doubt I'll miss anyone else, which is sort of sad.

The Fasten Seatbelts sign comes on and that's what I do, I fasten my seatbelt.

The End
by Margaret Bingel

Monday, 22nd December 2014

Nadia is sleeping next to her owner, kicking her legs as she dreams.

Ned, on the other hand, is wide awake, tapping his fingers to a tense rhythm.

Tap Tap Tap. His fingers march across his chest, like little toy soldiers.

Christmas is almost here. Even though he's way too old to believe in Santa, there's something about the one–week countdown to Christmas that really unsettles Ned. He can't sleep, he can barely eat, and he worries about whether or not he has the perfect gift for his mother. This year, Ned has bought her a new set of gloves, along with a card that says, 'Warm Hands, Warm Heart'.

He takes a deep breath and closes his eyes, envisioning his mother holding her boyfriend's hand with her newly–gloved one. He hopes Dr. Stanley likes the gift certificate to Nora's favorite restaurant he put in a blank card for him: that way his mother is guaranteed a good time. Ned knows that Dr. Stanley only wants to treat his mom like a lady, and he can respect that.

Ned reaches out to pet Nadia's back, her kicks dying with each stroke. He has set up a small tree on the floor for her to sleep under, and on Christmas morning he's going to hide dog treats in the branches. He found little candy cane−shaped snacks that he can't wait to feed her. He bought her a little hat too, which he rotates with the antlers and elf ears he makes her wear on their daily walks. Ned thinks it makes Nadia look more endearing, more lovable than she already is. She is such a good dog.

Waking up, Nadia looks at him with sleepy eyes.

"Come on, Girl, time to get up and go for a walk."

While Ned ties his shoelaces, his mind wanders back to Jeffery's party last Saturday, a big holiday bash where everyone brought their dogs and something to share. Ned brought soda, but forgot ice, so they had to use snow from outside. Jeffery was a really big sport about it, even warning people to not trust "dem drinks wid da yella snow!"

Shoes and coat on, and Nadia on her leash and wearing her elf ears, Ned steps outside, greeting the crisp, early morning cold. Through hell or 20 below, he takes his dog out for a walk. Ned lets Nadia choose the direction, and she pulls him east, toward the rising sun. Ned sees the icicles, so beautiful and prismatic this morning, glittering like perfect glass in the gaining light. Nadia pulls him along, sniffing anything, losing interest, and moving on.

What Ned doesn't see is a patch of black ice ahead. An unmoving slick of destiny, this puddle froze over the same spot where Ned fell almost a year ago. But there is too much for Ned to see and Nadia to sniff and sometimes you ignore what's coming up in front of you.

Ned places one foot right before the ice slick.

And sees his dog sprawled on her stomach, her paws slapping on the black ice. Ned bends down, puts his hand under her stomach and picks his dog up. Careful to side−step the black ice himself, he chastises, "You've got to be more careful, Girl. You never know when a slip becomes a fall."

Ned places Nadia on safer ground and tightening his grip on the end of her leash, they continue walking, east, towards the warming sun.

Beautiful Day
by Darryl Price

Tuesday, 23rd December 2014

It's a beautiful day, Doc. The kind of day that makes you feel like it's great to be alive, and that's what's so sad about it, I guess. I had a lot more to say to you in the lifetime, Doc, but I guess it'll have to wait. I'm not all that good at waiting around for something to happen.

Something has happened. Something that's very kind of big. So big, Doc, that it feels like the Empire State building in a room too small for even its shadow.

I don't want to say goodbye.

Goodbye doesn't work for someone you love so much. Does that surprise you, Doc? It shouldn't. It doesn't surprise me.

You brought that part of me back to life – the part that could feel things enough to love them, to care about what happens to them. How do you start to repay that with mere words?

If I thought they'd do the trick, Doc, I'd stay here all night and pour them constantly over your grave like soothing water.

But the truth is, they are only my selfish tears. I got a lot of tears for you today, Doc. Great big gobs of buckets of little girl tears that I can't seem to control right now.

Maybe I shouldn't have to.

You were my friend.

If you were here, Doc, I'd want nothing more than to shake your hand a good long time, but I can't. You always liked my words, so that's what I'm giving you now, Doc, one last time, the one thing you seemed to like about me the best. Right now I don't see it. I can't see anything. I'm blinded by this.

Thank you, my dear, dear friend, for being kind to me.

One last story, for old time's sake, Doc, just the way you like them: there once was two little boys who were very close childhood friends. They did everything together, went fishing, watched TV, talked about girls. You name it, they did it. The only problem was one of the little fellows was beginning to fade. He'd fade a little bit more each and every day. This alarmed his dearest friend to no end, but they never really spoke about it, but it was the really big question on everyone's mind, when would all this fading stop, and if it didn't stop soon where was it going to go to exactly, and to what lengths? The fading boy was fast becoming quite transparent in spots. Still he insisted on being treated like everyone else. Then one day all that was left were his hands, his smile, and his eyes. I guess I'm out of here, he exclaimed, and in a flash he was. The other little boy thought he should follow suit, but as hard as he tried, by scrunching up his own wet eyes and screaming real loud at the air, he couldn't make one bit of himself disappear. Over time the boy grew up. He never forgot his friend, he never would, and every now and then he still scrunches himself up in a sad attempt to wink out of the picture, too. Instead he got married and started a family of his own, who turned out to be all girls.

Good—bye.

Noel

by Teresa Burns Gunther

Wednesday, 24th December 2014

S usie's late as usual. I asked her last week if she wanted me
to get her a date. She laughed, more like a squeal and said,
"You don't do blind dates on Christmas Eve with family!"
It used to bother me the way she thought everything I said was
funny, but she says making people laugh is a gift. Who knew?
She tells me she's bringing her co—star.

"The *sleazy doctor*?" I tsked. She has terrible taste in men,
except for Steve, but he was gay and it didn't last.

"God, Rachel," Susie said. "It's just a role."

"But he has to know the part to play it."

"Well, I play a slutty nurse."

"True ..." I say. "You are not a nurse."

Susie squeaks my name in outrage then she makes these
funny noises. I ask if she's okay. She's laughing. She can't stop,
she's talking, gasping and snorting and all I can make out is
"crazy". I tell her to hang up and put the pedal to the metal, that
I hate tardiness and I have things to do.

I finish setting the table while Kevin, in my apron, is making
crostini and singing along to his cowboy music that is starting to

grow on me. Another surprise, just like him. I'm wearing the red cowboy boots he bought me with my mini–skirt he likes. Kevin sent me a link to an article about men who cook being sexy. Watching him now I have to agree. He looks good in the sweater I bought him, but my ruffled apron …? I pull another present from under my tree and make him open it. *Ho ho ho* he says, and hugs me. He likes everything I give him, even the gifts Susie says are dumb. But she's right about one thing: people love presents. I never knew how much I liked them myself. He pulls out the tuxedo apron and shouts a *yippe ki yay,* and whips off my ruffly one. I tell him I want to take him into my bedroom and … he shushes me, reminding me Mrs. Franklin is there. She sure is, listening to every word and grinning like a bad elf.

The doorbell rings. Gail, my officemate, hands me homemade brownies that look like she sat on them driving over. Her husband has a handlebar mustache. And people say I'm odd. He keeps pumping my hand saying how happy he is to meet me while Gail heads right in to check out my house.

Of course my father has to make an entrance with a big bouquet of flowers. He's wearing a shirt and tie and pulls a bottle of scotch from under his arm. Very good scotch! I thank him and let him kiss me and I'm surprised that I'm happy he's come. I introduce him to Mrs. Franklin who pats the couch next to her and says she'd like a word. *Give him hell,* I tell her. Dad, I agree to call him that tonight, pours me a drink and showers Mrs. Franklin with man attention, which makes me want suddenly to kiss him back. Mrs. F's cheeks glow, she pats her hair. She's flirting with my father! I serve the hors d'oeuvres. It's my first Christmas party, my last resolution of the year.

Kevin calls me to the door saying, "Larry and Joyce are here." I say So? Invite them in, but he tells me they have a surprise. They brought their plant with them? Weird. It's a baby tree, but they say it's a present for me! In a large pot, cobalt blue, my favorite color, with a big silver bow.

"It's a cutie tree, seedless tangies, your favorite!" Larry says, chest out, beaming, his arm around Joyce. He caught me pulling cuties off their tree once. Joyce hands me a bottle of wine, kisses my cheek and wishes me a *very very Merry Christmas!* I'm so surprised my eyes sting.

"Say thank you," Kevin says. I do and they all laugh.

"Please come in. Merry Christmas," I say twice before I can stop myself.

Everyone's talking and laughing and drinking. Stella is on her best behavior until she puts her head on Joyce's knee! I tell Stella *No!* but Larry says, "Its alright, Rach," and scratches behind Stella's ears which she loves. Kevin plays corny Christmas songs on his guitar and it's just too much. I look at them all, happy, in my apartment, and I can't breathe.

I slip outside to my front porch and focus on the lights, trying to breathe. I squint my eyes at the houses on my street lit up with color. Kevin helped me put white lights around my windows. Even the Jewish family down the street has lights, all blue holiday solidarity. I think back on a year ago, my miserable Christmas. Alone. What a year: 2014. So much has happened. I wonder what resolutions I'll make for 2015, but I can't imagine things getting better.

A car squeals to the curb and Susie hops out in a short glittery red dress. The *sleazy doctor* pays the driver. She introduces us. I start to tell him he looks shorter than on TV but stop myself. Susie looks worried.

"Why aren't you in your party?" Susie asks, looking worried. I tell her I'm waiting for her. I'm getting better at lying, an important part of people skills. She takes my hand and squeezes it as I lead them in.

Mrs. Franklin's delighted to meet Susie's date. She watches *As The Sperm Turns* religiously. She slides closer to my father and signals *sleazy doctor* to sit next to her. "My neighbor is a vamp," I say, caught up in the holiday cheer. Susie hoots and hugs me, tries to pick me up, staggering in her tiny heels.

"I have missed you, you nut!" she says and kisses my shoulder because she's such a shrimp, then hurries back to perch beside her sleazy doctor.

Kevin's watching me with those eyes. He's so handsome. He wraps his arms around me and nuzzles my neck. "Nice party," he whispers. And I am thinking this is happiness until I hear Stella barking then a riot of chicken noise, squawking and squealing in Larry and Joyce's garden.

"Who let my dog out?"

Morgana Malone and the Promise of 1000 Tomorrows
by Matt Potter

Thursday, 25th December 2014

"One big fantastic time we be having," Ludmilla says. Greasy grey–brown hair sticking out from under her bearskin hat, she sucks on her Christmas cigar. Clouds of eau de old–shoes–left–for–too–long–in–a–mouldy–wardrobe puff past my face.

"Christmas in July in June? No!" Now Ludmilla stomps her feet on the grey paving then throws her arms out like she's about to break into a show tune. "No no no! Christmas in December in Paris!"

Who would have thought?

Paris!

with Ludmilla!!

on Christmas Day!!!

Through my glasses, the high, wide entryway on the opposite side of the Louvre courtyard grows closer and closer with each stride.

I am not interested in why my former housemate and fortune teller is trying to be amusing. Nor am I interested in her wheezing or why she smokes celebratory cigars on Christmas Day. All I want to do is fasten the padlock on the famous Pont des Arts, then throw the key in the Seine. A photo of the padlock on the mesh railing glistening in the winter sun would be a bonus, but my camera is nestled in my suitcase back in our twin share at the Hotel d'Arabesque so I'm not counting on anything. It's just bridge, lock, throw. Anything else is a miracle.

I pick up speed, heels scuffing on the grey stones louder and louder and faster and faster.

The padlock weighs down the pocket of my puffy beige coat, banging a rhythm against my leg. And my fingertips are pink through fingerless gloves as I stride through the covered entryway, beneath hundreds of years of history (not that I'm interested in any of them), and step outside the Louvre. Ahead, I can see the famous pedestrian bridge and only metres away, catch a glimpse of the river.

"Wait!" Ludmilla calls out behind me. "Why you hurry? Bridge is falling down?"

I resist the urge to hurl a crack over my shoulder about this being Paris, not London, but western European bridge jokes are probably beyond her.

She's still yabbering on. "Stop! Why you be the bitch who stole Christmas?!"

God? fate? traffic? is with me as looking straight ahead I step off the kerb, no glance left or right, and onto the zebra crossing. My hair is short now, the leftover orange bob gone, chopped out, replaced with a brown and grey—streaked au naturel pixie cut, an early Christmas gift / holiday surprise / life—is—really—good celebration I gave myself two days ago. The puffy collar is warm against my neck as I hunker inside the coat.

And I'm charging, heels echoing on the black and white stripes and Ludmilla, who has kept me company ever since we left Adelaide at 10.35 last night, flying Emirates to Bahrain and then to Charles de Gaulle Airport, her gasps and wheezes and coughs grow fainter with each stride.

("No wondering no sheikhs are coming here," Ludmilla said as she sat beside me on the Emirates flight. "You looking like

Lebanese butcher." Then I shuddered as her hand ran up the back of my hair. "Your head is full of pricks.")

Bridge. Lock. Throw.

I will have a bruise on my thigh from the padlock bashing against it – the padlock's large and gold, though not gold just golden, maybe brass, maybe just wrapped in gold foil, I don't know but it *looks* gold and it has our names engraved on it.

Perhaps if I keep walking I can make London by sundown, or sundown tomorrow given it's winter and it gets dark by 5.00pm according to the internet.

Maybe I can escape Ludmilla.

Last night, I caught a cab to Adelaide Airport. *Meet me inside the international departure lounge,* Barry's text had said.

My armpits were sticky with the summer heat as I walked through the echoey terminal. And a grin spread across my face as all other travellers' noise faded away and I saw Barry standing outside the Customs check−in, in profile, high cheekbones on a thin face and short dark hair atop deep brown eyes.

But then he turned and it wasn't Barry, it was Grigor. His twin. Cheeks smoother than Barry's, nose finer than Barry's, forehead blander than Barry's … and he smiled when he saw me.

"Morgana," Grigor said, "it's good you could make it."

(What else was I going to do? On our two−week anniversary Barry bent down on one knee and said, deep brown eyes looking straight into mine, "Susan, you can sing carols at Christmas dinner for my homeless mates at the Whitmore Square Shelter, and I'll organise a screen for you to stand behind so you won't see their faces watching you while you sing" – which was tempting – "or we can fly to Paris on Christmas Eve and have croissants by the Seine on Christmas Day. You choose.")

"Where's Barry?" I asked. I would have fluffed my new hair except it's so short there isn't much to fluff and my hands were full holding my new puffy coat (bought just for Paris) and my carry—on luggage heavy with the three layers of winter clothes I'd packed to change into on the plane.

"In hospital," Grigor said, his deep brown eyes looking straight into mine. "Having a bit of a Christmas episode."

And then I saw Ludmilla standing behind Grigor, just as Grigor took my hand in his. Which was awkward as it was my left hand, half—buried under the puffy coat.

"Barry's fear of flying and of being trapped in confined spaces for a long time have taken their usual toll and he's having a rest on the psych ward," Grigor said. "It's a Christmas tradition. Although his fear of tinsel is new."

The puffy coat slid off my arm. "Barry flies to Paris every Christmas?" I looked down at the coat, pooled at my feet.

Grigor nodded. "He attempts to, yes. Barry's trip to Paris is a work in progress."

My hand slipped out of Grigor's clasp, just as Ludmilla peeked over his shoulder. "Barry ask me to Paris to go for him," she said.

"But I was with Barry this morning. We picked up my new passport together."

Grigor patted my hand. "Barry knows how to manage his illness. He knew weeks ago this would happen. And you can't fault his psychotherapy training, he recognises the signs."

"Barry give this for you," Ludmilla added, and handed me the padlock and key. The padlock was engraved with *Barry and Susan 25.12.14*, inside a heart. "He say, Tell Susan, Go! So I think you be this Susan."

I bent down to pick up the puffy coat. As I grabbed it, I saw a shiny new red and yellow overnight bag on the floor beside Ludmilla's feet. I stood up. "So this was all planned?"

"Go," Grigor said. "Don't even question it Morgana, just go." And then he added, "What other plans do you have for Christmas anyway?"

I did not expect to share my first visit to the most romantic city on Earth with Ludmilla. But maybe, while we were having our Christmas croissants by the Seine, I thought, I could give her the slip. Maybe push her in the river.

I opened my carry—on bag, took out my boarding pass and passport, and snapped it shut. I stepped around Ludmilla.

"I noticed your hair is no longer the colour of my favourite vegetable," Grigor said behind me.

I shuffled into the queue for Customs.

"It looks very attractive," Grigor said, "and not that masculine when you become used it."

Smiling at the woman in blue, I handed her my passport and boarding pass.

Thousands of padlocks glimmer in the muted sun.

Bridge. Lock. Throw.

My footsteps slow as I walk the Pont des Arts, wooden planks scuffing beneath my feet as I search the mesh railings for a spot for the padlock. The padlock in my coat pocket, banging against my leg and creating a bruise. The padlock Barry gave to Ludmilla, because he fears flying and cramped spaces and Christmas tinsel — haven't seen any tinsel in Paris so far, though I've really been too angry to look — to make the trip he'd planned for us both.

Bridge. Lock. Throw.

I thrust my hand inside the coat pocket. The padlock, key inside it, is cold against my fingertips. My eyes dart around the bridge, around the other pedestrians, searching searching searching the railings for a spot.

Bridge, lock, throw.

I spot a spot big enough to manoeuvre the lock into. Stepping up to the rail, I look over my shoulder towards the Louvre. Ludmilla, breasts bobbing, is heaving towards me.

This was supposed to be my moment with Barry.

bridge—lock—throw

And I don't want to share any more of this moment with Ludmilla.

bridgelockthrow

I'm standing on the bridge.

Bridge.

I pull the padlock out of my pocket, gold key still wedged inside it.

Lock.

The padlock is open so I snap it shut. I pull out the key. I see *Barry and Susan 25.12.14*, surrounded by the engraved heart.

Throw.

I swing my arm back and throw the padlock over the rail.

Throw.

I throw the padlock off the bridge.

Throw.

I throw the padlock off the bridge and into the river.

Throw.

I don't even hear the faintest plop as the padlock hits the water.

I look down. The key glimmers in my hand.

My head snaps back towards the Louvre. Ludmilla has stopped walking. Her mouth is open. Perhaps she is dribbling, or perhaps it is too cold to dribble. Either way, she is not saying anything and she is standing stock still, fur boots nailed to the wooden planks of the Pont des Arts.

My mouth is open too. But the insides of my cheeks are dry and my tongue is cold, so I close my lips and wait, arms by my sides. I think I might be pouting.

Burrowing into the neck of my coat again, I pull my bottom lip over my top lip and breathe out, my mouth a funnel, fogging up my glasses.

I can't see through the fog.

In Telluride
by Gary Percesepe

Friday, 26th December 2014

Gabrielle decided to meet me for Christmas back in Telluride, with Anna in tow. My ski partner and former college roommate Henry joined us, bringing his girlfriend Kate, thinking this was too good to miss. We booked a room in Mountain Village and settled in for the week. Christmas was weird, alternative and swell. Presents all around. The next day Gabrielle wants to ski backcountry, so we leave Anna to ski with Henry and Kate, and head out. We're an hour from Telluride when my phone rings. It's Henry.

"Gary, Frankie's here. She got in early this morning. I picked her up from the airport. Where in the goddamn hell are you? It's the fucking day after Christmas and you kidnapped the kid's mother? Are you fucking kidding me?"

"What the fuck! What is she doing there?"

"How the fuck should I know, man!"

Henry lowers his voice, and whispers, "She's your wife, remember? Where are you guys?"

"We're getting close to Ouray. Is she there next to you?" I ask.

"What do you think?"

"Put her on," I say.

Gabrielle glances over at me from behind the wheel. She accelerates smartly into a curve, pushing my shoulder into the car door. I grab the handle above the window and drop the phone.

I pick the phone off the floor. Its silver skin is nicked from a hundred drops. The small screen is smudged with fingerprints.

"Frankie," I say.

"Gary?"

"Yes."

"Did you drop the phone?"

"Yes. I'm sorry. We hit a curve."

"Is Gabrielle driving?"

"Yes."

Silence on the line. "Listen," she says. "Is it OK if I stay in the hotel suite with you all tonight?"

I hesitate a second too long. I register the mistake, but hesitate some more, compounding the error. Then say, enthusiastically, "Of course." Which sounds idiotic.

Gabrielle pokes me in the ribs. I frown and cover the mouthpiece. "What," I say to her.

"What?" says Frankie.

"Nothing. Sorry. Sure, it's OK. It's not a problem at all. I want you to."

"Good," Frankie says. "Because there are no rooms in Telluride over the holiday. You guys are the local Hilton."

Gabrielle pokes me again. "What's she saying?" she asks.

I cover the mouthpiece again. "We're the Hilton," I say.

"No fucking kidding," Gabrielle says.

Gabrielle arches an immaculate blonde eyebrow.

"Ask her where she's going to sleep," Gabrielle says to me.

I make a quizzical face, and then cover the phone up again.

"Jesus! Gary. We don't want a No Room At The Inn scenario, do we. Which room does she want? There's not enough room for everyone to have their own room, duh. Does she expect to sleep with you or what? How does she feel about the couch?"

I shake my head, no. As in, there is no way I am asking that question on this phone.

Silence again on the other end.

Gabrielle takes the phone. She checks the Motorola's bars for reception, and then quietly kills the call with one manicured finger. But she goes on talking into the mouthpiece.

"Hi, Frankie, this is Gabrielle Marceau. I've kidnapped your husband but I'm returning him in a few hours, intact for the most part. Do you still want him?"

She snaps the phone shut and drops it in my lap. Then she steers the Range Rover into the lighted island of a Conoco station.

"Do we need gas?"

When that gets no response I say I'm sorry.

"Yes. Never the fucking less, we got us a housing situation here," Gabrielle says. She ticks the ash from her cigarette.

I am officially rethinking my lose—your—life—in—someone— else—for—a—while theory.

We pull into Telluride, opting to take the stairs up to the suite. I slip the key card into the slot, and push the heavy door open. It's quiet inside, and there is no one to greet us. It smells like vanilla. A single candle burns on the coffee table. We walk into the kitchen. Frankie stands at the stove. She's wearing a boyfriend blazer over a sequined T—shirt, black jeans and boots, stirring a saucepan with a whisk. She wipes her hands on her jeans, and then holds one out for Gabrielle to shake. "Hi, I'm Frankie," she says. She pecks me on the cheek.

"What are you cooking?" Gabrielle asks.

"Baked ziti, garlic bread," Frankie says. "Something simple. Tossed salad. A bottle of good Chianti."

"You've been busy," Gabrielle says.

"There's a great market in town. Henry and the others are still out skiing. I thought it would be fun to eat in tonight, instead of going into town. Did you guys eat?"

"We had some lunch on the road, thanks."

There's a saucepan simmering on the stove. "What's this?" I ask.

Frankie's pan is filled with white cream. She's got a carton of eggs on the counter, flour, salt, some oranges, and a box of chocolate. There's an open bottle of single malt scotch next to the stove. Her blazer is a gray pinstripe with narrow lapels.

"It looks like an orange and chocolate soufflé you've got going," Gabrielle says.

"That's my favorite," I say.

"I know this one," Gabrielle says. "I have it in a book somewhere at home in Greenwich. Here, let me help you."

Gabrielle takes the carton of eggs. She opens two or three cabinet doors and finds a mixing bowl. She starts separating the eggs. The yokes slide from their cool white shells into the clear Pyrex bowl.

Frankie uncaps the scotch. She opens the refrigerator and takes out a tray of ice. Then she shakes her head, and puts the ice back. She grabs three tall glasses and places them in turn under the refrigerator's ice maker. The ice clinks into the glasses in a satisfying way. She asks the two of us if we want water with our scotch. We both shake our heads.

"Salut!" I say.

We tap glasses.

A few minutes later we tap again with new ice, then repeat.

Frankie laughs at something. She begins to whip the egg yokes. She has a Cameron Diaz laugh, filled with mischief and surprise. I stare at her ass in the black jeans. I am pretty sure they are new jeans. Ditto the boyfriend blazer. The boots I recognize. Around her neck and in her ears are diamonds I gave her from previous Christmases.

Next to her, Gabrielle whips the egg whites. I refresh our drinks. We work as a team. The cream bubbles to the top of the saucepan. Frankie lifts it off the gas burner. Gabrielle adds the eggs. Frankie pours in cognac, and then bends low to smell. "Mmmm," she says.

Gabrielle shreds the rind of an orange while I melt bittersweet and semisweet chocolate in a small saucepan. Frankie comes up and dips her finger in the pan and puts her finger to her mouth. The tips of her fingernails are pure white, a French manicure.

The egg whites are foamy. Frankie adds sugar, beating the mixture until it is stiff. She folds the whites into the chocolate mixture. Gabrielle dips two orangey fingers into the chocolate. Frankie grabs her hand and pulls the chocolate finger to her lips. Then she turns to me and says, "What a charming family you've found, Gary. *La jeune fille et sa belle mere.*"

Which for some reason cracks Gabrielle up. She goes into fits of laughter, braying loudly, bent at the waist. Her blonde hair scrapes the saucepan, dipping the ends brown. Which makes us all laugh harder. Frankie reaches in and smears Gabrielle's cover girl face with chocolate. Gabrielle hand wrestles her, their chocolate fingers laced together, and backs her down over the counter. She's got three inches on Frankie, a longer reach, and, I'd guess, ten pounds. I shake my head and pour a fourth glass of scotch.

There's an old Woody Allen line, where he says, "I was always better in my art than I was in my life." In my California filmmaking days I used to think about that line. I watch these two women's performance, if that's what it is, and think about shooting them, in this kitchen light, my head a whirring camera. But the light's not right and I'm starting to lose my buzz. They're just playing, but I don't feel part of the game.

I know I'll immediately regret it but I ask anyway. "So Frankie, how was the bag boy?"

Frankie looks past Gabrielle's shoulder, at me. Gabrielle starts to pull away but Frankie keeps hold of her hands, and pulls her back in. "He wasn't bad, actually, but I'd rather kiss her." Then she does.

This time I laugh. And then I do shoot them in that light, a medium two shot, until they release. It's a stage kiss, but it's effective. I pour us all another drink.

De–Cloned
by Nathaniel Tower

Saturday, 27th December 2014

Samford is lying in a comfortable bed, a woman's arm draped over his chest. He wakes up stiff, unaccustomed to sleeping on his back. He glances at the woman and smiles to himself. Gently, he removes her arm from his chest and scoots himself off the bed, trying not to wake her. Clothes and used condoms are scattered all over the floor. Samford tiptoes around the room like he is maneuvering through a mine field.

"What are you doing?" the woman asks just as he steps into the master bathroom.

Samford stops in the doorway and glances back at her. "I'm taking a leak," he says. "But I'll be back for whatever you want in a second."

"Hurry up. I need a lot." She blows him a kiss. "In fact, I need it all."

Samford laughs and turns in a hurry, not wanting her to see his sudden erection even though she's obviously had it inside her plenty. He closes the bathroom door and struggles through a boner piss, the urine spraying in an uneven stream he can barely control. His dark yellow pee squirts onto the white porcelain, making him aware of his severe dehydration. He doesn't bother flushing or shaking off the drips.

Samford steps to the sink, his boner starting to shrink back to its small flaccid counterpart. Instead of washing his hands, he reaches for a pickle jar sitting next to the soap dispenser. He holds the jar up in the light, staring at the long metal chip inside. His lips mouth the long string of numbers.

Still holding the jar, he peeks out of the bathroom. The woman is uncovered, a hand gently caressing her crotch. Samford watches her until she notices.

"Knock it off, you perv." She doesn't stop touching herself.

"Want something bigger in there?" he asks from the doorway.

"Come give me everything you've got."

Samford drops the jar on the carpeted floor. As he bounds to the bed, his asshole seems to wink goodbye at the strange chip trapped in the jar. In a matter of seconds, his boner has returned to its full force. For the first time in his life, Samford knows exactly what to do with himself.

Gifts

by Kimberlee Smith

Sunday, 28th December 2014

In the kitchen, Mum has a tangled bunch of limp snakes in her hands. Taipan, Western Rattlers, and Death Adders. She shakes them loose into a cardboard box that has 'MASTER BEDROOM' written across it in square black letters, then looks at Etheline, who toddles toward her. Mum's expression – pinched brow, pursed lips – says *Don't come near. This is grandmum's work.* Etheline stretches out her arm, cups her hand as if it's cradling something precious, and then blows at her palm while she looks at her grandmum. Her eyes are pure golden amber; the sun shining into their kitchen has contracted her pupils to slits as thin as papercuts. She purses her lips and blows a kiss at Mum, and Mum raises her hands in front of her mouth, catches the kiss, and mimes gobbling it up. Then she turns back to the terrariums and collects two more handfuls of dead snakes. Those are the last.

Etheline stands one foot away from the meter–wide telly screen; so close her hair is full of static from the electricity. She has gone back to watching *The Wiggles*. It is a daylong marathon, interrupted only by having her diaper changed, her bottle filled with cordial, or plucking a Tim Tam from the box on the floor of the family room, which is peppered with crumbs. She is transfixed while Mum continues with the unpleasantries of this day, none of which includes properly cleaning the house. There is a nearly-empty bottle of gin on the kitchen table and a pot in the sink with spaghetti sauce crusted on it. Two plates with wormlike noodles glued to them sit on the draining board.

Dorothy the Dinosaur is dancing up a storm: kicking her foot as high as it will go, which means the actor's cumbersome costume only allows it to go straight at the knee and no higher. She and the Wiggle in the purple shirt have their arms locked and are imitating dancers at the Moulin Rouge doing the can-can. The pirate jumps across the stage and plucks two large red feathers from his hat and hands one to each of them. They wave them around, apparently working hard to look silly, but it seems as if they're actually having fun. But they are actors, acting.

Etheline swings the belt from her bathrobe above her head like a cowboy lassoing. She shakes her other wrist, and the bracelet her daddy made for her from real snake rattles ticks, fast and noisy, like live snakes rattling. In the other room, Mum hears it over the cacophony blasting from the telly. She's unnerved by the sound of rattles these days. She's physically shaking when she hears it. And her eye twitches. She clenches her teeth. But she says nothing and lets the bub carry on, playing with the only friends she has, the ones on the television she's been watching, day in, day out, for weeks.

It's been just that long since she and Etheline returned from their road trip to find Brother Tom, using up a 36-pack of adult diapers, only stopping for petrol and to feed and change the bub. She kept herself going on caffeine pills. She didn't stop to sleep.

Now she's crippling herself with booze and alienation.

Mum's been in a catatonic state ever since she encountered Brother Tom's new family, helping deliver his wife Alice's newborn son and bury its stillborn twin, Jacaranda, my new baby here in the afterworld. I'm not sure she'll ever come out of it. She moves around like she's had a lobotomy. A botched one. She doesn't think or feel any more, other than yammering to herself and shooting poisonous looks at Etheline. Resentment.

Disappointment. Jealousy. She's accepting the minimum to get by: minimum sleep, minimum air, food, and substituting liquor for water. Always.

I try to reach out to her but she's not listening.

The bub often cries a little too long. She simmers in acidic diapers for hours, her tiny pink throat becoming swollen and pimply. Dry and angry. Her eyes don't spend tears. She cries now. And her eyes stay dry. She is sunburned. And what makes me crazy more than anything else, is that she has discovered fear. She acknowledges she is alone in her world.

What I want Mum to know is that we all have been renewed through a death. Even though I'm gone from the living world, and Brother Tom is gone from her life, Mum is no exception. Etheline can replace me, the daughter she lost. I've received the greatest gift I've ever known by way of the greatest tragedy of someone else's life. Jacaranda is not just my half–sister, she's my daughter. I wish there were a way for me to save Mum. And thank Alice.

I'm here for the long haul, looking over them all.

Lots of Ways to Die
by Vanessa Weibler Paris

Monday, 29th December 2014

There are lots of ways to die.

You can die of embarrassment. Seeing a woman in a doctor's waiting room, just the two of you there. Words are exchanged, with little sense and less connection, but you imagine yourself telling the story later on. To parents, friends, eventually children. "I was watching her read her magazine. I didn't even mean to say it out loud. I'm pretty sure she thought I was nuts!" Meet cute made meet−cuter by counterpoint. "I didn't even notice him; I really didn't. And then he suddenly burst out with − what was it? Something about January? I still don't really get it. But yes, nuts. I kind of thought he was."

Instead, the reality: she looks at you not just like you're nuts, but like you're a creep. Like you disgust her, with your bony body. You see her take a quick step back, nearly stumbling, and her head jolt back on its neck as though it's the latest dance move. You imagine dancing with her, high−school style, your hands faux−lding her waist while her arms circle your neck. 'Stairway to Heaven' is playing, and it's eight minutes long, long. But she looks at you, magazine forgotten, pupils pinpointing, heeled feet shuffling backwards, no story writing for friends, family, eventually children, and there, you die of embarrassment.

You can die of virginity. Can you? You turn pragmatic, looking for statistics to normalize you. "WELL," you imagine tossing off in a not–quite–condescending tone, "According to the Centers for Disease Control and Prevention, the average age Americans lose their virginities, defined here as vaginal sexual intercourse, is 17.1 for both men and women." You take a sip of your water, small so as not to choke, swallow and add, "The CDC also reports that virgins make up 12.3 percent of females and 14.3 percent of males aged 20 to 24."

"Your father and I saved ourselves," your mother whispers as you wish you were anywhere else but here hearing anything else but this, "we saved ourselves for marriage, for our wedding night, so special it was so special because we waited." But they were 22, your parents, you're nearly 30, none of this helps, and so you die of virginity.

You can die of diet, not that you ever would because you've spent your life trying to gain, but when your only work friends are women decades older who spend every day every week every month every year trying to lose that last five ten fifteen fifty pounds, you hear the angst fourfold. *If I have to eat another iceberg lettuce salad today, I will DIE.* Dead of diet. *If I don't lose at least half a pound after eating nothing but celery and poached skinless boneless chicken breasts all week, I will DIE.* Diet, die.

You can die of not aging. You can die young. You find yourself born on February 29, and then you don't have a birthday and don't have a birthday and don't have a birthday and then finally have a birthday, and then it starts all over again, for the rest of your life. You're nearly legal to drink but not quite qualified for kindergarten.

You can't die of being ugly on the inside, rupturing and infecting like sepsis. If you could, Iris would be long gone.

You can't die of being full of holes, nostrils and navels and marrow and pores. If you could, we'd all be dead.

You can die of water intoxication.

(You can.)

You can die of loss, of regret, of sadness.

(Can you?)

You can starve to death. Not accidentally, not circumstantially: *purposefully*. In the name of art. As a creative exercise. As a debt owed Iris. As a *favor*.

You can reverse things spectacularly, guzzling and binging, to show that you won't be an experiment, an exhibit, a pièce de résistance. You can Prader−Willi your way out, drown in a bottle of Dasani. A cure for curation.

Or .... you can just die.

Rewind the year that changed everything. Regain a bit of hope, not too much. Find your family. Find your friends. Make amends for what you gave up with her, for her.

Go back to being Slim Jim. Iris−free. Go back to that life.

Have beers with your buddies, when they can escape from their wives.

Crunch salad with the work ladies, and tell them they look thinner even when they don't.

Tend Dougie's grave, and apologize for not being there at the end, knowing you're already forgiven.

Eat cake on your birthday, every four years.

Blow out the candles, smiling faces flickering around you, wishing for nothing more or less than you already have.

All these thoughts float through your head as you sink back onto the white sheet, and the white pillow, and watch the white ceiling blur in and blur out, and your breathing slows ... and slows ...... and .... slows .... and your lungs rattle ....

And then you, eventually, uneventfully ..... die.

Endings and Beginnings
by Joanne Jagoda

Tuesday, 30th December 2014

"Hey Cass. Aren't you done? We should be at Denise's soon. She wants to leave by 2 so we make it to Tahoe before dark."

"Yeah, I'm almost finished."

"You're bringing way too much stuff."

"I know Rob, but I can't decide what to take."

"Why are you in such a crappy mood?"

"I'm uh, not in a crappy mood."

"Yeah, you are. You've been so quiet the last couple of days. I know you, and you can't fool me. Stop with the packing and you're picking your cuticles."

Cassie blurts out, "I did something sneaky ... behind Mom's back."

"Ooo ... this sounds too good. You, Cassie, the Perfect Donaldson Daughter??? Come on Cass, *what* did you do?"

"Rob, I'm serious. Mom got a letter and I hid it from her."

"Go on."

Cass digs under a pile of clothing in her top dresser drawer. "Here ... it came a week ago. I was curious when I saw the envelope."

Robin picks it up and notices the postmark from Scotland. "I don't get it. Mom doesn't know anyone in Scotland."

"Yeah, she does. Read it. "

Dear Annie,

I never regretted anything in my life but meeting you. I've lived one lie after another and never cared. The time I spent with you I saw what a real relationship could be. You trusted me, but I used you in the worst way.

I'm living in a tiny village near Dundee in Scotland. It's green and peaceful. I hike every day. It's not the Napa Valley but the countryside is lovely. You might be surprised that I'm working in a pub, minding my own business. For the first time in a long time I'm staying in one place. I have a small flat not fancy, but I don't mind it. I just wish I didn't have to be looking over my shoulder. I hope my former employers will grow tired of looking for me.

Annie, come to see me. I want you to meet the real me. I'm still discovering that person every day. I have sent you an open ticket. Write back to me. Give us a chance to start all over.

Yours, D

Robin raises her voice. "Shit Cass. He wants her to come to Scotland? What did you do with the ticket? That bastard!"

"I hid it in my drawer. I didn't want her to see it."

"Would she go to be with him? Leave us?"

"I don't know, Rob. I know she loves Sandy but ... part of her thinks about Damon. One night she didn't see me but I found her looking at the pictures they took on their Napa Valley trip. She was crying hard, this sad silent cry."

"Do you think she cares about him? How could she after what he did to her?"

"I don't know, but I suppose he was exciting and not at all like Dad or Sandy. Rob, I didn't want her to get ... uh ... confused or tempted. I was afraid she might do it ... go to him, leave us. I guess that's crazy."

130

"Cassie, you did the right thing. He was a sneaky, ruthless asshole. He would have hurt you or worse to get Grandpa's plans for the ransom. Now, you got him back good. Mom doesn't need to know about the letter and the ticket. It's our secret. Give me the ticket. Let me tear it up."

"Here it is. I feel so much better since I told you, sis."

"And I have a secret too, Cass."

"What Rob? You've got a huge grin on your face. Tell me right now."

"I wasn't supposed to but what the hell. Sandy and I went shopping for Mom last week. We picked out a gorgeous sapphire and diamond ring. He's going to propose on New Year's Eve, tomorrow night.

"Rob, I knew it. I knew it! Let's jump on the bed. Yahoo. There's your cell, Rob. It's Mom."

"Shhh, Cass. Don't say anything to Mom."

"Alo−HA, Mom. How's Maui?"

"Hi Rob. Ummm, this resort is luxurious … palm trees everywhere, atrium in the lobby, parrots in cages and white sand beaches. We have an ocean view suite and are sitting on our balcony now. I'm being very spoiled by Sandy. Going down for brunch in a minute, then we are having massages. When are you leaving for Tahoe?"

"Soon. Cassie has to finish packing."

"Promise me you won't be driving around tomorrow night. New Year's Eve is crazy in Tahoe … and the roads are slick and people drink and …"

"Mom, you've told us a hundred times. Bye, chill, have a good time. Say hi to Sandy."

"Bye Hon. 2015 will be a better year for all of us, I know it for sure. Love you guys."

Both girls yell into the phone, "HAPPY NEW YEAR!!"

§

It's 9PM in a little village in Scotland. It is raining hard. Damon Southeby is about to leave for his shift at the pub. He opens his mailbox at the end of the lane for the fourth time today, looking for a letter from Anne Donaldson. The mailbox is empty. He curses and slams the mailbox shut then takes out a disposable cell phone and dials a number.

"Yeah, it's me. I'll take the job. I'm ready to get back to it in 2015. Tell me the details."

A Road Through the Desert
by h. l. nelson

Wednesday, 31st December 2014

Dear Diary,

Right now, I'm in a car, hurtling through a hot desert. Temple sometimes smiles at me like she's the Louise to my Thelma. But we're not alone.

We've been driving this way for what seems like forever. But I know that can't be so. I remember Anne's party as if we were still there. The Christmas tree aflame, the ice sculpture melting in the blaze, and bodies writhing everywhere.

But let me rewind a bit so I can tell the story.

To take my mind off Brandon and the kids, Robin, Julie, and I helped Anne every week in November and December until the party. We were good little helpers to Anne's face, but took every opportunity we could to undermine Winter Wondersnatch. Without alcohol, Robin was even funnier, giving the caterer and designer the incorrect address, moving the specially–placed poinsettias and topiaries of mistletoe to the wrong places, then we'd watch Anne blow her top. I even hid her $400 cold cream. It has roe in it, for god's sake.

Besides that little incident, Anne thought we were so nice and helpful. It was all a ruse. We felt sure there was no helping Anne, and that she was going to get exactly what she needed.

Finally the big day arrived, and all of us showed up early to help get the tables set up, supervise the caterers (Yes, she ended up hiring multiples, "in case one of them screwed up"), and to lug the ice sculptures into their proper places. The centerpiece was a seven−foot installation, a huge chunk of ice that Anne had insisted the sculptor chisel into a family of swans. I'd handled that call myself. It was to remain curtained until the "Big Reveal," and I'd assured Anne that I checked it myself, that it was just beautiful and perfect for the party. She'd beamed, and continued barking orders at the caterers and florist, while the designer fumed. Many of them looked like they wished she was dead. I wished then that they could be there for the party, thought how bright their smiles would be after.

We also helped dump all the pounds of Swiss chocolate into the "chocolate mountain" that Anne had bought for the occasion. Most people just rent these things, but not Anne. I may have had quite a bit of the sticky, sweet stuff, shh. We had to turn the thing on several hours before the party even started, because it all had to melt in "cascading rivulets" down the "rocks" like Anne wanted.

Oh, and we spent hours putting together little waterproof votive candles, because Anne wanted to float them in the pool. Even though no one would be using the pool. It was December, for god's sake. Anyway, an hour before everyone was to arrive, we had to manually light each candle and set them afloat. I asked her why the staff couldn't help, and she said she didn't "trust those morons to do anything correctly." I wondered why the hell she hadn't fired them yet.

I'd handled the invitations. Or, rather, I stole several of the extras, then took them to the bar where I'd met Temple. Lo and behold, she was already there. And, of course, she said she knew I'd be coming. Nothing surprised me anymore where Temple was concerned. She said with a wink that she'd make sure her friends were invited.

Winter Wonderbread was looking like it'd be quite a good time.

Guests finally started arriving around 6 p.m., and Anne was still upstairs dressing. I let them in, showed them to the refreshments, and made sure the 12—piece string orchestra began their set. I poured the contents of a small thermos, secured from Temple the day prior, into the Waterford punch bowl while everyone else was occupied.

Julie stayed near the bar and refreshments, making sure guests were getting a large helping of the punch, which she was hawking as "Anne's own special recipe" and Robin near the large ice sculpture. It would not be unveiled until Anne had made her grand entrance, around 7 p.m. She'd given us explicit instructions.

A few things happened right about the time Anne descended like a queen down the massive staircase and through the French doors, trailed by a Korean lady—in—waiting, who held Anne's drinks, fetched her tiny bites of food, fixed her taped—up tits, and any other small whim Anne wanted fulfilled. The orchestra had begun 'The Swan' by Saint—Saens. So Anne was posing there, in a fur—trimmed (faux, but very real—looking, so real that she may have just *said* it was faux) short, deep—red jacket with beadwork, over a luxurious silver silk gown. She had on custom Cinderella slippers. Pretty, yes, but ridiculous. When she was there in front of the French doors, Temple and her friends came pouring out of the great room. Temple said, "Nice gown, Mama," grinned, and hip—bumped her way to me.

Anne's and the other guests' jaws dropped as the parade of what appeared to be prostitutes, druggies, and other unsavory types descended on the gathering. For a moment, no one knew what to do. Temple enveloped me in a big hug, smelling like wet earth and spices, and said, "*Now* it's about to be a party up in here." She smiled and turned away, but then turned back and, holding up a small black device, added, "Oh, and this little thing'll cut their cell reception so we can really party." Then she sashayed her tight–clothed ass away from me, to the beat of the cello and violin ensemble.

I saw Anne trying to escape inside, probably to find her cell or use her alarm system to ring the police, so I fast–walked after her, convinced her I would take care of it, then ushered her back outside to sit in the chair of honor next to the large ice sculpture. Temple and a thin woman in a leopard–print mini and a blonde wig were waltzing together with very serious faces, then they cracked up and gyrated instead.

I fixed a glass of punch, grabbed the mic from the orchestra, finger–motioned them to finish up their song, and strolled over to the sculpture, where Robin and Julie jittered, both smiling nervously, ready to pull the curtain aside.

Anne, in the seat of honor by the covered sculpture, leaned toward me and whispered fiercely, "Are the police on the way?" I nodded yes. "Thank GOD. I don't know how these people found out about Winter Wonderland, but this is the WORST."

"I know, it's terrible. Here, a drink to take the edge off. I put something special in it for you." I handed her a glass of punch and winked. She looked down at it, then up at me, so I smiled warmly at her. I'm pretty sure she figured I'd popped in a Xanax or two, because she downed the entire glass. For the tiniest moment, I felt bad for the spiked punch and for Anne, with her rich, but empty life. I saw Temple across the pool, standing tall and majestic near the chocolate mountain, her eyes closed and lips moving. I turned my attention back to Anne, and in that moment, I think I really saw her. Watching her scared face, in a flash of insight, I realized how very much Anne and I had in common. I didn't want to unveil the sculpture anymore. I knew then that Anne was already suffering, that I was suffering, and I no longer wanted to contribute to our shared pain.

That's when Robin gave the signal, and she and Julie pulled back the curtain. There stood, at seven feet tall, an incredible likeness of Anne, completely naked and looking back over her shoulder, a perfectly pink–colored circle of ice around her cold bleached anus.

There was complete silence for maybe ten seconds. Then someone vomited right into the chocolate mountain, and every person except the four of us ladies and the one who puked burst into uproarious laughter. Anne's mouth was almost big enough for me to crawl into, she was so aghast. She turned her incredulous expression toward me. By now, there were multiple guests puking. Some in the pool, others on each other, on the lawn and topiaries. It was the drug, coming out full force. "You," she said. "You did this." She looked like she would kill me.

I said nothing, just waited.

With that, Anne punched me in the nose so hard I fell on the sculpture. Right onto Ice Anne's back thighs, breaking her frigid legs, her freezing torso falling on me, knocking the breath out of my lungs as it shattered against my body and the lawn. The ice shards cut into my scalp and back as Anne jumped on top of me, slapping and punching me while screaming. Through Anne's thrashing arms, I saw Robin and Julie running to my rescue, but I managed to wave them off. They stopped and took in the improbable scene.

I had become the epitome of everything I'd always hated. I wasn't mad at Anne. I realized all of this while she was beating my face and chest with her fists. My blood spattered her silk dress and faux fur jacket and I started laughing. It was so ludicrous, all of it.

Anne stopped hitting me and I sat up. We both breathed in ragged gasps. The freezing air gave me clarity. I looked to her and, smiling, leaned over and gave her a big hug. She softened against me and hugged me in return. Then we both started laughing hysterically. Flat–out, no holds barred, belly–grabbing laughter. In the midst of it, she stopped and threw up all over her gown.

"Let's jump in," I said, nodding toward the pool. "Come on, ladies!" I yelled at Robin and Julie as I tugged my dress over my head while running toward the pool.

I cannonballed in, hit bottom, and surged back to the top. Robin, Julie, and Anne plunged in, in that order. We'd disturbed some of the floating votives, but others were still flickering, bobbing on the concussive waves. Beyond the pool, all around us, people were silent with big eyes, yelling, or vomiting. Many were curled into fetal positions on the lawn. Some of the unsavories were roving around, asking the guests if they were okay.

"I accept! I accept!" Anne yelled in the pool, and I knew her trip had begun.

"Are you okay?" Robin asked me, dog–paddling nearby.

I thought for a moment, feeling my swiftly–closing right eye and throbbing nose and jaw. "Yes. Absolutely." She and Julie looked relieved, and we watched the pandemonium as a group of the guests stripped off their gowns and tuxes and ran across the lawn and jumped over the fire pit. One of the naked men picked up a potted Christmas tree, lugged it to the bonfire, and tossed it in. The tinsel went up in sparks and sent plumes of black smoke toward the open sky. It was then that I saw Temple, backlit by the roaring tree, her arms spread wide and teeth gleaming in the night. Then she was leaning over the side of the pool, handing the three of us glasses filled with the pure drug mixture. She stroked my hair, her pupils reflecting the tiny votive flames. Robin, Julie, and I clinked our glasses together. I said, "To friends."

Temple, Robin, Julie, Anne, and I have been in this car, in the desert, ever since. We've all changed, in our own ways. Robin is so funny and vibrant, no longer angry. Julie has more gumption, speaks her mind like she never did before. They're both strong, fierce. Anne and I, we paint together. We create like twin artists, playing off each other. Not to be too hippy–dippy about it, but now she is like the other half of my soul. I guess hippy−dippy is okay sometimes, because I have seen many things over the last year, and I know there really is no going back. Not in the way you might think.

Dear diary, I don't need you anymore. I am complete now. But, I am completing you with this entry. I couldn't leave you hanging.

What I want to tell you is that us women will drive through this steaming desert forever, leaving a billow of dust behind. The road will stretch ahead, always, stretching us out beyond ourselves, and circling us back. That is not what is in question. What is in question is if we can make it through the heat and sand, tired and lost, until we find our way home.

Pedal to the metal,

Joan Colderman

Authors

Rachel Ambrose

is a twenty–something fiction writer from Connecticut. Her favorite season is winter, she enjoys well–made Manhattans, and she loves Southern fiction. Her work has appeared in *Crack the Spine*, *Exiles Literary Magazine*, and *The Colton Review*. She is currently at work on her second novel and she blogs at http://victorywhiskeyjuliet.tumblr.com.

Lynn Beighley

is a fiction writer stuck in a technical book writer's body. Her stories often involve deeply flawed characters and the unsatisfying meshing of the virtual and actual world. She has an MFA in Creative Writing and currently has 16 books published.

Margaret Bingel

is just a writer, living in Manchester, New Hampshire. She spends her time working at her father's beer store, art modeling, and writing (when she can). She doesn't have a website or a blog yet, but who knows, maybe she'll have one in the future.

Guilie Castillo-Oriard

is a Mexican writer currently exiled in the island of Curaçao. She misses Mexican food and Mexican *amabilidad*, but the laissez-faire attitude and the beaches of the Caribbean are fair exchange. Plus, the bounty of cultural diversity inspires great culture-clash fiction. Guilie is currently revising and editing her first novel. Her short stories have appeared in *Fiction 365*, *Lady Ink Magazine* and *Pure Slush*. She blogs at http://guilie-castillo-oriard.blogspot.com.

John Wentworth Chapin

lives and writes in Baltimore, where he is too frequently starting Project B before finishing Project A. John writes non-fiction as well as fiction. Find him at http://johnwentworthchapin.com.

James Claffey

hails from County Westmeath, Ireland, and lives on an avocado ranch in Carpinteria, CA with his family. He is the author of a collection of short fiction, *Blood a Cold Blue*. His website can be found at http://jamesclaffey.com.

Gay Degani

has published online and in print including *The Best of Every Day Fiction* editions and her own collection, *Pomegranate Stories*. She is the founder-editor emeritus of EDF's *Flash Fiction Chronicles*, a staff editor at *Smokelong Quarterly*, and blogs at http://wordsinplace.blogspot.com where a list of her work can be found. She's had two stories nominated for Pushcart consideration and won the eleventh Annual Glass Woman Prize for her flash piece, *Something about L.A.*

Michelle Elvy

is an editor and writer who has meandered from the shores of the Chesapeake to New Zealand's Bay of Islands. Michelle has published poetry, short stories and non–fiction about travel, faraway places, food, motorcycling, slow travel, the kindness of strangers and raising children in unusual places for numerous literary journals and magazines in the US, Canada, Australasia, the UK and Europe. She edits at *Flash Frontier: An Adventure in Short Fiction* and *Blue Five Notebook*. She can also be found regularly at *Awkword Paper Cut*. More about manuscript assessment and Michelle's take on editing and writing can be found at http://michelleelvy.com.

Gloria Garfunkel

is a psychologist and writer with a Ph.D. from Harvard University in Psychology and Social Relations. A former psychotherapist, she has published many stories in literary journals and anthologies.

Teresa Burns Gunther

has had fiction and non–fiction appear in numerous literary journals and most recently in *Northwind Magazine*, *Bookslut* and *Best New Writing 2012*. Teresa is the Editor of *The Lakeside*, an online literary magazine, and she founded Lakeshore Writers Workshop in Oakland, California where she leads creative writing workshops and classes and works one–on–one with writers. You can find more information and links to her work at http://www.teresaburnsgunther.com/.

Gill Hoffs

lives with her family and an ever–dwindling supply of Nutella in the North of England. Find Gill on Facebook or as @gillhoffs on twitter, email her a dirty joke at gillhoffs@hotmail.co.uk, or leave a clean comment at http://gillhoffs.wordpress.com/. *Wild: a collection* was published by *Pure Slush Books* in 2012. Her non-fiction book *The Sinking of RMS Tayleur: the Lost Story of the Victorian Titanic* is out now from *Pen & Sword*. Feel free to send her chocolate.

Joanne Jagoda

of Oakland, California, took an inspiring writing workshop after retiring in 2009, and launched on a long-postponed creative writing journey. Since discovering her passion for writing, she has worked non-stop on short stories, poetry and non-fiction. Her work has appeared in a number of e-zines and print anthologies, including *Pure Slush* and *Idea Gems Magazine*, and she was a poet of the month for a Jewish news weekly in Northern California. When not taking writing and poetry classes, Joanne enjoys being a writer-coach for ninth graders, Zumba, and visiting her three grandchildren in Jerusalem.

Len Kuntz

is a writer from Washington State and an editor at the (currently on hiatus) online literary magazine *Metazen*. His work appears widely in print and online, and you can find more of his work at http://lenkuntz.blogspot.com.

Sally-Anne Macomber

was born and raised in Toronto, Canada, and studied journalism at Concordia University in Montreal. Her work on high fashion and the demise of haute couture has appeared in various online and print publications in both Europe and North America. She turned to writing flash fiction in 2010, and hasn't looked back.

Jessica McHugh

is an author of speculative fiction that spans the genre from horror and alternate history to epic fantasy. A member of the Horror Writers Association and a 2013 Pulp Ark nominee, she has devoted herself to novels, short stories, poetry, and playwriting. Jessica has had thirteen books published in five years, including the bestselling *Rabbits in the Garden*, *The Sky: The World* and the gritty coming—of—age thriller, *PINS*. More info on her speculations and publications can be found at http://www.jessicamchughbooks.com.

Gwendolyn Joyce Mintz

is a fiction writer and aspiring photographer. Her work has appeared in various online and print publications. In other incarnations, Mintz is a writing instructor, a teddy bear maker and somebody's grandmother.

h. l. nelson

is Founding Editor / Executive Director of *Cease, Cows* lit mag and a former sidewalk mannequin. Pub credits: *PANK, Hobart, Connotation Press, Metazen, Drunk Monkeys, Red Fez, Bartleby Snopes.* She's also editing an anthology which includes stories by Aimee Bender, Roxane Gay, Lindsay Hunter and other fierce women writers. Her MFA is currently kicking her ass. Tell her what you're wearing: heather@hlnelson.com.

Mandy Nicol

grew up in Melbourne, Australia and made a tree change to country Victoria in the mid—nineties — the decade, not her age. She has various animals including a flockette of pet sheep that are thankful for her vegaquarian habits. She writes short stories and loves flash fiction. *Pure Slush* is the first venue to publish her work.

Derek Osborne

lives in eastern Pennsylvania. His work has appeared in *Boston Literary Magazine, Bartleby Snopes, Literary Orphans, The Linnet's Wings, Pure Slush* and many others. To read more visit http://gertrudesflat.blogspot.com, or you can email him at derekosborne1@gmail.com.

Vanessa Weibler Paris

lives in Erie, Pa., with a guy, a girl, a boy, a bunny rabbit and a dog. She writes things both real (for work) and pretend (for fun). Her favorite things include hot peppers, bad puns, small—world stories, and tales with a twist at the end.

Gary Percesepe

is Associate Editor at *New World Writing* (formerly *Mississippi Review*) and a Contributor at *The Nervous Breakdown*. Author of four books in philosophy, Percesepe's poetry, fiction, essays, and interviews have appeared in *Story Quarterly, N + 1, Salon, Mississippi Review, The Millions, Brevity, PANK, Metazen, The Brooklyner*, and other places. His collection of short stories, *Why I Did the Grocery Girl*, is forthcoming from Aqueous Books. His poetry collection *falling* and his flash fiction collection *itch* were published by *Pure Slush Books* in late 2013. He has taught at Saint Louis University, Wittenberg University, and University of Dayton. He lives in Buffalo, New York.

Matt Potter

is an Australian—born writer who keeps a part of his psyche in Berlin. Matt has been published in various places online, and he is, rather amazingly, also the founding editor of *Pure Slush*. You can find more of his work at http://mattcpotter.webs.com/.

Darryl Price

was born in Kentucky and educated at Thomas More College. A founding member of L. Jack Roth's Yellow Pages Poets, he has published dozens of chapbooks, and his poems have appeared in many journals. He currently edits *Olentangy Review* with his wife Melissa.

Stephen V. Ramey

is an American author from New Castle, Pennsylvania. His work has appeared in many places, including *The Doctor TJ Eckleburg Review*, *The Journal of Compressed Creative Arts*, and *A Capella Zoo*. *Glass Animals*, his first collection of (very) short fiction is available from *Pure Slush Books*. Find him and more of his work at his website: http://www.stephenvramey.com.

Shane Simmons

is a self—confessed coffee shop writer who believes that regardless of quality, each paragraph penned should be rewarded with sweet treats (cake, muffins, Belgian waffles, etc). London—born, he ran away to Glasgow ten years ago. Since then he has expanded his waistline and he now blogs at http://scribblingsimmons.wordpress.com/.

Kimberlee Smith

is a writer whose poetry, essays, fiction, and creative non—fiction have been published in numerous literary journals and anthologies. She was awarded a residency to the Jentel Arts Program in 2013. She received her MA in English from the University of Sydney, a certificate in the Creative Writing Program through UCLA, and her BA in Journalism from the University of Southern California. She can do a headstand on a trampoline, kill a chook, and make hard cider from the apples in her orchard.

Andrew Stancek

was born in Bratislava and saw Russian tanks occupying his homeland. His dreams of circuses and ice cream, flying and lion–taming, miracle and romance have appeared in print in *LA Review*, *Windsor Review* and *New Sun Rising: Stories for Japan*. Among the many online publications featuring his work are *Every Day Fiction*, *Gemini Magazine* (Flash Fiction Contest Grand Prize Winner), *fwriction*, *r.kv.r.y.* quarterly literary journal, *Tin House*, *Flash Fiction Chronicles*, *The Linnet's Wings*, *Connotation Press*, *THIS Literary Magazine*, *LA Review*, *Windsor Review*, *Thrice Fiction Magazine*, *New Sun Rising*, and *Pure Slush*.

Susan Tepper

is the author of four published books of fiction and a chapbook of poetry. Her most recent title *The Merrill Diaries* (*Pure Slush Books*, July 2013) is a Novel in Stories that follow a young woman's adventures in love and lust on two continents, spanning a decade. Tepper has received nine Pushcart nominations, and one for the Pulitzer Prize in fiction. You can visit her website here: http://www.susantepper.com.

Nathaniel Tower

lives in the Twin Cities with his wife and daughter. After teaching high school English for nine years, he decided to pursue a career in writing / publishing / editing. His fiction has appeared in over two hundred online and print journals. His first collection of fiction, *Nagging Wives, Foolish Husbands*, was released in 2014 through *Martian Lit*. Nathaniel is the founding and managing editor of *Bartleby Snopes Literary Magazine and Press*. You can find out more about Nathaniel at http://nathanieltower.wordpress.com.

Townsend Walker

lives in San Francisco. His stories have been published in over fifty literary journals and included in seven anthologies. One story won the SLO NightWriters story contest. Two were nominated for the PEN / O. Henry Award. Four were performed at the New Short Fiction Series in Hollywood. He is associate editor at *Grey Sparrow Journal*. During a career in finance he published three books, on foreign exchange, derivatives and portfolio management. Educated at Georgetown, NYU and Stanford, you can find his website at http://www.townsendwalker.com.

Michael Webb

is continually surprised anyone is interested in what he has to say. He blogs at http://innocentsaccidentshints.blogspot.com.

Other volumes in the *2014* series
from Pure Slush
Visit the Pure Slush Store:
http://pureslush.webs.com/store.htm

June 2014 Vol. 6
ISBN: 978–1–925101–49–2

July 2014 Vol. 7
ISBN: 978–1–925101–37–9

August 2014 Vol. 8
ISBN: 978–1–925101–40–9

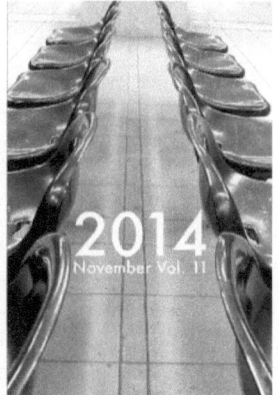

September 2014 Vol. 9
ISBN: 978–1–925101–43–0

October 2014 Vol. 10
ISBN: 978–1–925101–50–8

Nov'ber 2014 Vol. 11
ISBN: 978–1–925101–53–9